in the
SHADE
of the
SUGAR
MAPLE

FOUR GENERATIONS OF LEGACY
FROM A KENTUCKY CEMETERY

in the SHADE *of the* SUGAR MAPLE

a novella

JENNY SMITH

-PUBLICATIONS-

In the Shade of the Sugar Maple
© 2026 by Jenny Smith

Published by Significant Publications. Louisville, Kentucky.
All rights reserved. No part of this book may be reproduced; stored in a retrieval system, including but not limited to generative AI training systems; or transmitted in any form or by any means—for example, electronic, mechanical, photocopy, recording, or otherwise—without the publisher's prior written permission or by license agreement. The only exception is brief quotations in printed reviews.

This is a work of historical fiction. Certain characters, places, and events are based on historical fact, while others are the product of the author's imagination. When historical figures appear, they are presented in a fictional context; their words and actions are interpreted imaginatively.

Cover Design by Carpe Librum Book Design
Interior Design by Jenneth Leed, JennethLeed.com

ISBN: 978-1-7370867-8-9, print
ISBN: 978-1-7370867-9-6, epub

For my dad, who passed on the legacy of reading, learning, and telling a good story.

CONTENTS

Part 1: Thomas and Susanna Graham	11
Part 2: Mary Wilcox	37
Part 3: Robert Hillaire Wilcox	61
Author's Note	99
Historical Notes	103
Acknowledgements	111
Discussion Guide	113
Resources	115
About the Author	117

This story reflects the language and attitudes of its historical period. Certain terms and expressions used by the characters are now considered outdated or offensive. They are included here only to preserve historical accuracy and authenticity, and no disrespect is intended.

Part 1

THOMAS AND SUSANNA GRAHAM

Thomas Graham
September 18, 1797
Chestnut Ridge on the Forbes Road in western Pennsylvania

Thomas Graham's body ached as the cold from the ground seeped through the oilcloth as he lay near the fire. Rain pattered on the tarp of their lean-to, not quite covering the steady sound of breathing coming from his younger brother James and brother-in-law Eli. His wife and sister retired in the relative comfort and privacy of the Conestoga wagon with its canvas covering.

The group had finished day eight of walking seven to ten miles a day on nothing more than a stony path. The journey was enough to make both man and woman bone weary. The wagon, which carried their earthly belongings, only offered a single lazy seat, which slid out from the bottom of the wagon for an exhausted walker. His lively sister, Lizzie, had uncharacteristically occupied that spot the best part of each day. Thomas assured himself that Lizzie was simply tired from walking.

Most nights the party of five had found respite in cabins or barns of hospitable strangers, but they had no guarantee of comfort. On the third night of the hundred-mile journey from their hometown of Bedford, Pennsylvania, to Pittsburgh, the party agreed to stay outside in the shelter of the wagon and lean-to shelters. While a generous family had offered them shelter, the small cabin overflowed with an abundance of children—and excessive filth.

The burden of responsibility weighed on Thomas that night. Susanna, his wife of ten years, entrusted him with their future. She had gone along with his harebrained idea to move the family and most of their possessions to the Kentucky frontier for its fertile land, but now Thomas was discovering the reality was far more difficult than his dreams.

He thought back on the past several years. Thomas had distilled his surplus corn and rye into whiskey, which brought higher profits than grain and was easier to transport. With the extra income, he'd saved enough money to move west—along with selling the land he'd inherited from his father to his brother Moses. As the oldest son, Moses had received the best of the Graham family's land.

When the new federal government passed a whiskey tax, western Pennsylvania erupted in an uproar. As President Washington and thirteen thousand militiamen arrived in Bedford to quell the insurrection, Thomas kept a low profile and didn't get caught up in the unrest, though he disagreed with the tax.

Susanna was ever a source of constant support. She had caught his eye from an early age with her bold auburn hair and honey eyes, but it was her fierce determination that snagged his heart. Even then, she could be as stubborn as a pack mule. He chuckled, remembering their first fight after

Susanna cooked a meal that proved inedible. She'd taken his plate, stomped outside, and tossed the food to the chickens. "It's good enough for these birds. You'd better plan on sleeping with them tonight while you're at it."

"Did I hear you laugh over there?" Eli propped up on an elbow to look at Thomas in the light of the fire.

"Oh, pondering about what I've gotten us into. And why you and James are foolish enough to follow me," Thomas said.

"It's Susanna we trust, not you." Eli laughed, then grew serious. "That and your brother Elias claims the land is as good as gold in Kentucky territory."

"We've a long way to go with hardships still to come." Thomas sighed, expressing his doubt and fear.

"It'll be worth the trouble." Eli nodded his head with assurance despite a yawn that swept through his body. Thomas watched him lie back down and wrap the wool blanket over his shoulders.

Thomas shivered. He was cold, yes, but it was more than that. Now that they were in the open, all he could think about were the dangers they could face in the mountains and all the way down the Ohio River.

Susanna Graham
October 3, 1797
On the Ohio River near Point Pleasant, Virginia

Susanna portioned out the rations for their family of five. She prepared a meal of coffee with milk, cold ham, bread, butter, biscuits, and cheese, still amazed that a fire hearth on the flatboat kept them comfortable at night and allowed her to cook while floating downstream. The flatboat was a plenty comfortable way to travel by river. Certainly better than taking the Wilderness Road down south through the mountains. At forty feet long, the boat had a large covered room, spacious enough to partition into two sleeping areas for the travelers and boatmen.

In the four days since they'd pushed from the Monongahela to the Ohio River, Susanna had become accustomed to the soft rolling as they navigated downstream. Late summer rains meant they didn't have to wait for the river levels to rise; low levels often hampered travelers this time of year. Susanna shook her head as she remembered how Thomas had spent his days and nights worrying that they'd lose precious time and resources waiting on rainfall. Despite all of Thomas's strengths, his biggest shortcoming was his desire to dominate nature, as if he were God himself.

As she swept the hot coals off the Dutch oven, lifted its lid, and placed the biscuits on a serving plate, Susanna marveled at how the group had covered over seventy miles since they passed William Tinton's settlement at Belleville and the rapid waters downstream from there yesterday. Lizzie, Susanna's sister-in-law, seemed less in awe of the river and more peaked from the swaying flatboat. Each day at dawn, Susanna noticed Lizzie ate sparingly and retched what little she had managed to eat. While Susanna enjoyed standing at the front of the flatboat, breathing in the fresh fall air, Lizzie cowered in the relative safety of the living quarters, so unlike her normally energetic self. But for Susanna, the power of the river under her feet and the glory of the colors that burst forth from both banks of the river invigorated her. The majesty of creation never ceased to amaze her.

"Supper ready?" Thomas poked his head into the living area, cheeks rosy and golden hair mussed from the cool outside air.

"Just finished. I even made biscuits." Susanna grinned as Thomas shuffled in, hugged her from behind, and pecked a kiss on her cheek.

"You know how to bake the way into a man's heart, love," Thomas whispered into her ear. She leaned into her husband, relishing the warmth and strength of his embrace.

Susanna loved her family, but she surely did miss these private moments with her husband. The Graham and Stillwell families were a close-knit group. Susannah and her paternal cousin, Eli Stillwell had each married a Graham sibling, binding the two families twice over—Eli to Lizzie and Susanna to Thomas. James, yet unmarried, looked forward not only to a fertile piece of land but also the possibility of finding a pretty wife in Kentucky.

Susanna sighed, disappointed that they needed to rejoin the group. "I best get the meal served. Now help me take the food out to the others."

Upon seeing Thomas and Susanna carrying the victuals, the deckhands and owner of the boat, who had become trusted travel companions, sat down at a makeshift table with the family and enjoyed the meal. The conversation revolved around the fine weather and river conditions that allowed the flatboat to steadily move downstream.

"In two days, we'll arrive at Maysville," the flatboat owner said. "I'll offload supplies to trade, and we'll resupply before continuing downstream to Louisville." He brushed crumbs off his lap and stood. "Mrs. Graham, thank you for the fixings. Mighty good meal for a man on the river."

Eli cleared his throat and licked his fingers from the buttered biscuits. "Thomas, Susanna, there's something Lizzie and I want to talk with you about." He shifted and grabbed Lizzie's hand. "Well, you see, Lizzie and I are going to get off at Maysville."

Susanna pulled her attention from gathering dishes to Eli's unexpected declaration. Get off? She sat down, weak-kneed with apprehension.

"I imagine we'll all get off for a bit," Thomas said.

"No, Thomas. We're going to settle in Maysville. Lizzie is expecting a child, and we both think it's best to live in a more established town. With Maysville being a good trading post, I can work as a blacksmith and provide for Lizzie and the babe."

Susanna bit back the ache in her heart and forced a smile, now recognizing her sister-in-law's queasiness and fatigue for what it was. Susanna had been ten years married and still waited for a child to survive outside her womb. "Lizzie, congratulations," Susanna said with as much felicity as she could muster.

But Thomas thrust to his feet and stalked to the far end of the flatboat, before swinging around. "How can you do this? This wasn't what we'd planned!" Thomas growled as he turned his back on the others and stared out at the river with his fists clenched.

Susanna looked from her husband to Eli and Lizzie, compassion teeming for her husband who'd planned every step of this passage. Then she wondered if Thomas's anger could be disguising a pang of sadness over the couple's good news. Susanna unconsciously placed her hand over her empty womb. If she were honest, disappointment—no, jealousy—churned in her heart as much as if she were tossed into the murky waters of the Ohio. She shook her head and took a breath to clear her thoughts. She wouldn't be snared by envy. "You know his temper burns hot. He'll cool down once he has a moment to think."

Thomas would come around, but could she? Susanna yearned for a private place to cry out her unspoken grief to God.

Thomas
December 8, 1797
Fairmount, Kentucky

Two months had passed since Thomas and Eli had parted on good terms in Maysville. He couldn't fault his brother-in-law for wanting to keep Lizzie and the baby safe. It might have been his decision, too, if he and Susanna had received that very blessing. Now, they would have family in the trade hub, where goods would be shipped to Lexington over the Maysville Road. The town was, in fact, the largest Thomas had seen on the Ohio since Pittsburgh.

When they left Maysville, the fall showers had kept water levels up to make the trip down the Ohio to Louisville in only three days. The settlement of Louisville was small—just one thousand souls. The port at Beargrass Creek was sufficient and provided easy access to buy a wagon and horses for the thirteen-mile trek from Louisville to Fairmount, where his brother Elias lived.

This morning, Thomas had signed and paid for the land. His eagle eyes surveyed every tree and stone marking the boundaries of his one hundred acres on the banks of Floyds Fork. Maple and sycamore trees stood at the southeast corner of the land, and walnut, sugar maple, beech, black locust, and mighty elm trees dotted its borders. Most of the land was thick with virgin soil. Clearing the property would take several seasons, but Thomas had expected that, prepared for it too.

Even with a house of little ones, Elias and his wife, Anna, welcomed Thomas, Susanna, and James with open arms. Despite the warm greeting, the tight quarters lit an urgency in Thomas. He'd risen at dawn to meet the local clerk along with William and Sally Thompson, the sellers of the one hundred acres. Thomas handed over forty-eight pounds, signed his name on the deed, and took possession of his land. *Their* land. He and Susanna would make a life for themselves and any children God might bless them with. It wasn't his family's land, but Thomas would clear and farm this land and pass it down to his children.

After surveying the land, he arrived at the small log cabin that would serve as their temporary home. Thomas heard Susanna and several of the local women inside, chirping away like a host of sparrows, as they cleaned and dusted. But Susanna was no sparrow. Among the women, she stood out bright as a yellow warbler singing its *sweet-sweet-sweet-sweet* song. The humble cabin would do for this winter. But come spring, the men would build more spacious accommodations with the logs they'd already felled and peeled.

As he approached the door, the women laughed in response to something Susanna said. Thomas ducked through the door, squinting into the low light and smirking at his wife. "Now don't believe everything she says. She was one of the best storytellers in Bedford County."

"Look who's telling fibs now." Susanna swatted him with her rag. "I may tell a good story, but it'll always be a true one."

Thomas chuckled as he knelt on one knee and inspected the fireplace. "Looks like I'll need to clean the flue if we don't want smoke this winter. But it'll do." He nodded and stood to face the women. "If we want to get back for the night, we'd best head out now. Tomorrow, I'll drive the wagon over with our belongings, and we can make ourselves a home."

Susanna
April 1799
Fairmount, Kentucky

"Thomas," Susanna called from the bedroom, her left hand resting on her aching lower back while the other hand grasped the steady walnut bed they had brought with them from Bedford two years ago. When Susanna didn't receive a reply, she bellowed again, "Thomas, where in tarnation are you?"

The door squeaked on its hinges and heavy footsteps followed. "Thomas, go fetch Mrs. Welsh."

"Why ever would you want me to get Mrs. Welsh?" Thomas walked into the room, realization crossing his face. "Oh, Susanna. It's time?"

"Thomas, you don't want to cross me right now." Susanna flashed him a glare and let out a groan louder than spring thunder.

"I'll fetch her." He placed his hand over hers, squeezed it, and ran from the house.

After years of waiting, Susanna was finally going to have the child she and Thomas had hoped for. During the past two years, they had settled into the newly built cabin. The neighbors—the Thixtons, the Welshes, and the Hayses—as well as Thomas's brothers James and Elias, had built a new cabin after their first winter. By faith, they built the cabin with a second floor, holding out hope for children. By late that summer, Susanna felt all the familiar signs of being with child. Again. She could only pray that she wouldn't lose another.

Again, a contraction wracked her body with pain. With each breath, she exhaled fear and inhaled hope and expectation. "God, let this wee one live."

Susanna reclined in bed and held the newborn while she watched Thomas gaze at their daughter. "Can it really be?" She caressed the baby's soft peachy hair.

"Hello, Elizabeth," Thomas cooed.

Susanna smiled, loving the name they'd chosen. "A strong name."

"Like her mother." Thomas looked at Susanna with a crooked grin, tears puddling in the corners of his eyes. "Susanna, I'll do everything in my power to provide for you and Elizabeth."

Thomas
February 7, 1812
Fairmount, Kentucky

From the warmth of his bed, Thomas heard their hogs grunting and squealing in the distant field. He turned over and attempted to fall back asleep when the chickens squawked in the hen house. Then their prized heifer let out a deep moo from the barn. Comfortable in the cabin despite the freezing temperatures outside, Thomas was grateful for the warmth of the fire and the logs that insulated their home. Although he didn't want to go check on the animals, his good sense—and concern for his livelihood—won out. He rolled out of bed, trying not to wake Susanna.

"Where are you going this time of night?" Susanna murmured.

Thomas lit a candle and looked at the silver pocket watch he'd received upon his father's death. "It's three thirty. Something has the animals riled up. Go back to sleep," he whispered, not wanting to wake eighteen-month-old Susie, settled in a cradle next to her mother. The older girls—Elizabeth, now almost thirteen, and seven-year-old Mary—slept upstairs in the loft. Other babies, born too early to survive, lay in tiny graves near a small sugar maple tree. Thomas pulled on his trousers and layered a woolen jacket over his long linen shirt. He slipped into the living area and grabbed his smoothbore musket from above the hearth, then headed out the door.

Clouds prevented the moon from lighting his way, and a light mist burned cold as it hit his face. The animals continued to raise a ruckus. He could only hope a cougar hadn't attacked his hogs, hen house, or milk cow.

As Thomas neared the barn to check on the heifer, a deep rumbling filled the air, growing louder by the second. Soon, Thomas felt the earth tremble under his feet while his stomach lurched with dread. Another earthquake.

Over the past three months, a series of earthquakes and aftershocks had shaken the region. If newspapers could be trusted, the quakes had been felt as far away as Boston and Washington, DC. Experience told Thomas the safest place to be was the cabin since the logs absorbed the tremors. He shuffled on trembling legs back to the cabin. Susanna met him at the door, holding Susie in one arm while the other two girls clutched their mother.

"Papa," Susie cried and lunged for Thomas. He grabbed her and encircled his youngest daughter in a protective hug, while Mary ran and threw her arms around his waist. "I don't like the rumbles, Pa!"

"I know, darling." He knelt and wiped away her tears. "Let's go sit by the fire until the earth settles."

Elizabeth, ever her mother's helper, picked up Mary and comforted her. Thomas stumbled toward Susanna, placed his hand at the curve of her back, and guided his wife to the multicolored braided rug in front of the fireplace. Then he moved the few knickknacks from the mantle to the floor.

As the ground continued its moaning, minute after terrifying minute, dishes rattled in the walnut cupboard, while the cherry table tiptoed across the wood floor.

Susanna recited scripture as a prayer. "God is our refuge and strength, a very present help in trouble. Therefore will not we fear, though the earth be removed, and though the mountains be carried into the midst of the sea; Though the waters thereof roar and be troubled, though the mountains shake with the swelling thereof."

Thomas had watched her memorize the psalm after the Methodist circuit rider had preached this passage to his small congregation—a group that had doubled in number since the earthquakes began in December.

Finally, a quarter of an hour after it began, the earth and its creatures fell silent.

Susanna sighed. "Best grab Susie's cradle and some blankets. We'll sleep together until daybreak." She yawned. "I expect aftershocks."

Thomas nodded in agreement. He placed Susie into her mother's arms and settled the blankets and the cradle near the fireplace so the family could attempt to rest until dawn.

Two days later, the family walked one mile, crossing Bardstown Pike, to the Thixtons' house where several families gathered. Not a particularly religious man, Thomas still abided by his wife's wishes to worship with neighbors on the Sabbath. If nothing else, he was happy to talk with the other men. And this week, the traveling minister from the Salt River circuit wasn't in, which meant that Mr. Thixton led the small group in hymns and prayer. The time was blessedly short before the group was ready for the meal.

Thomas sat next to Mr. Ash who passed him a plate filled with corn muffins. As Thomas chose a muffin, spread butter and poured maple syrup on top, Mr. Ash leaned in. "News reached me yesterday that Guthrie's house did not fare well."

"I heard the same," Thomas said. "He and the Presbyterians planned to meet at another congregant's home this morning on that account, just to be safe." James Guthrie was a fixture in the area, one of the earliest settlers, and had served in the Revolution. His house was built of stones taken from Cedar Creek—one of the few such houses in the area.

Little Mary, overhearing her father's conversation, whispered into Susanna's ear, "Isn't Mr. Guthrie the man with the scary face?"

Thomas chuckled, but Susanna shook her head at him in disapproval. "That's not kind, Mary. Mr. Guthrie can't help the way his face looks. He was shot in the face during an Indian raid." Mary's eyes opened wide with astonishment. While Thomas had seen the Shawnee and Cherokee passing through the land now and again, for the most part the tribes had been pushed north and west of their area.

Mr. Ash continued, "Those stone buildings don't withstand the earthquakes as well as wood. He and Eunice suffered a great deal of damage to their home."

"Is it habitable?" William Thixton asked.

"It is. The fireplace needs shoring up and the mortar repaired. But I'd hate to see what another quake might do."

Voices murmured in understanding. After the constant rolling underfoot over the last months, no one wanted to feel, hear, or see another earthquake. This force of nature demonstrated that Thomas had little control of his family's future. And he didn't like that one bit.

Thomas
May 1817
Fairmount, Kentucky

The late May sun warmed Thomas's back as he dropped two or three kernels of corn into the tilled earth. He furrowed his brow, pondering the late start due to the rains. Once again, nature had trifled with his plans. Mary and Susie followed behind him, while Susanna worked in the house. Hoes in hand, they covered this year's hoped-for harvest with the rich earth, singing and chatting to make the tedious chore less monotonous.

Thomas thought back to late March when the snow had melted and the land brought forth the bright green promise of new life. Chipping sparrows and purple martins sang as they built their nests, and the does—alongside the season's earliest fawns—dotted the land. However, the brightness of spring was short-lived.

The following week had thundered with heavy clouds, hollering wind, and pounding hail, which damaged outbuildings and livestock alike. And the rain. Never-ending rain. Floyds Fork spilled over its banks and onto Thomas's fields. Never had he been so grateful for his brother's wisdom to build their cabin on the high land, even though the trek from the house to the fields was steep and precarious, with a two-hundred-foot descent down to the fields. The flooding had pushed back planting season until the waters receded and the soil dried out. No reason to chance root rot and disease.

Despite the setback, this year Thomas hoped to see a crop of two hundred bushels of corn. The backbreaking work of plowing the land near Floyds Fork took him and Susanna from sunup to sundown on several continuous days. Thomas had even rented Robert Ash's ox and wood plow since they didn't have their own.

His thoughts drifted to the first year they had plowed the land. Thomas had steadied the plow, turning over the loamy soil, rich with silt, sand, and clay. Susanna had guided the ox, up and back, up and back, along the long six-inch-wide rows until the six acres of soil was tilled. It took them one week of grueling effort to complete six acres.

In the past ten years, he had also cleared enough land for a small garden to sustain the family with potatoes, beans, and squash. Thomas raised a few hogs and salt-cured the meat. Out in the dairy he had built, Susanna made butter and cheese with the extra milk the dairy cow produced. The chickens laid more eggs than the family could eat, so they traded those, along with the butter and cheese, for salt, cloth, and other necessities.

"Hello!"

A voice calling from the cabin forced Thomas back into the present. He looked toward the house where two women stood, the younger one waving her hand in greeting.

"Who's that up near the house?" Susie shaded her eyes from the sun.

"Why, it's Elizabeth with your mother." Thomas smiled as he watched the distant figure lift her skirts and romp down the steep hill, following the earthen path that led to the field. Two years ago, he had given his consent for Elizabeth to marry. She had been young—two years younger than when he and Susanna had married—but Elizabeth had assured her father that she loved Wilkinson Gregsby and desired to marry him.

Susie tossed her hoe to the ground and ran toward her big sister.

"Elizabeth!" Susie threw her arms around her sister, who welcomed her little sister's hug. "I've missed you! It's not fair that Uncle Wilkinson took you away from us." Susie stepped back and placed her hands on her hips with a huff. "Why can't you be like the new Mrs. Thixton and move right close to us?"

"Darling, Mrs. Thixton married Mr. Thixton. It's only right that she moved into his house across Bardstown Pike. Wives move to live with their husbands, not the other way around." Elizabeth tousled Susie's hair, then greeted Mary and bound toward Thomas.

He hugged his daughter and held on a little longer than normal. Thomas saw a weariness in Elizabeth that had stolen the bloom of youth from his firstborn. Was everything all right in her marriage?

"Papa, you worry so." Elizabeth looked into his eyes. Thomas grimaced when he realized she saw the concern on his face. "I came to help with the planting. I can drop kernels, and Susie can hoe with me while Mary pairs up with you. We'll cover the land twice as quickly."

And allow for time away from her husband. Thomas frowned, concerned for all that might be hidden in her reason for the eight-mile trip from Jeffersontown.

"It's good to see you, Elizabeth. Pardon, *Mrs. Gregsby*." He smiled, though his heart ached with worry. "The next bag of seed is over there. Grab it and let's get this work done."

Thomas sat on the porch that evening, whittling wood while his wife and daughters chatted. He thought about all the blood, sweat, and tears he had poured into this land for almost twenty years. Clearing the land had been laborious. Building the detached kitchen, dairy, and springhouse for Susanna had only been possible with the help of family and neighbors. Farming the land had been no easier. Battling the extreme Kentucky weather had been harrowing as well. The winter of 1806 had been so cold that the mighty Ohio had frozen over. Another summer, he lost most of the crop when not a cloud nor drop of rain had been seen for months.

However, Thomas could feel it in his bones, sore as they might be from the day's work, that his effort and determination would leave a legacy for his children. At least that was his hope. Though the earthquake had rattled the ground underneath him, it hadn't shaken his belief that he could make something worth passing down to generations.

Yet, who would the next generation be since he and Susanna had no son? Certainly not Wilkinson Gregsby—who rarely visited. But maybe Mary or Susie would marry a man worthy of that legacy.

Susanna
December 14, 1827
Fairmount, Kentucky

Susanna sighed with satisfaction and admired the holly and ivy that decorated the inside of their cabin. Bright red berries peeked out from all corners of the room and set a festive mood for the wedding. Today, her youngest daughter, Susie, would marry Mr. William Wilcox.

"Mama, you need to sit down." Mary grasped Susanna's hand and tugged her to the wooden bench in the corner of the main room.

"You treat me like an invalid, Mary." Susanna exhaled deeply while she took a seat. "It does look beautiful, doesn't it?"

"It does." Mary squeezed her mother's hand. "When is Papa to arrive with William?" Mary was nearly as excited as her sister for the day's events, but Elizabeth? Her cheerfulness was more subdued as a result of loss and heartache; nonetheless, she anticipated the upcoming nuptials.

"Your father and William will be here any moment, and the guests should arrive by noon for the ceremony." Susanna stood, wanting to lay eyes on all of her daughters. "Now let's check on the bride."

As the pair entered the sleeping room, Elizabeth pushed a final pin into Susie's chignon, leaving a few golden ringlets to frame her rosy cheeks. The bride wore her best dress, a shade of blue that matched both the sky on a cloudless summer day and her eyes.

"Isn't she a vision, Mama?" Elizabeth swiped away a joy-filled tear. Susanna hadn't seen her oldest daughter so alive since she'd moved back home with them a year ago. The past few years had been heavy with heartache for Elizabeth. And it was no wonder with not one but two husbands buried and gone, and no children from either marriage.

"She sure is." Susanna blotted the corners of her eyes with a kerchief. "Susie, dear, I wish you all the joy that your father and I have shared. William certainly seems worthy of you."

Two years ago, Susanna couldn't have expected that the man who purchased the sixty-five acres bordering Big Run and Bardstown Pike just north of their property would soon be her son-in-law. Thomas had certainly fought the idea of a marriage from the beginning. "The man is growing an orchard!" Thomas had spat. "Why not something steady with less risk? But peaches? Only a deranged man would plant an orchard!"

Susanna chuckled that her husband had overlooked the fact that many farmers in the area owned profitable orchards. "Thomas, if I had listened to my father, I wouldn't be standing by your side. Give the man a chance." She arched her eyebrows, challenging her husband's logic.

While William Wilcox planted his orchard and waited with anticipation for his first harvest in the next few years, he had proved helpful on their farm. She and Thomas were now sixty-one years old. Thomas still dearly loved the land and willed it to bear more and more for his family's benefit. Often to his own—and his family's—detriment, the man seemed to believe he could govern creation itself. But they were both slowing down, whether or not he wanted to acknowledge that fact. William was a blessing they hadn't known they needed.

The sound of the front door creaking open brought Susanna back to the present. "Girls, I'd like to pray together before the wedding. Shall we?"

The women gathered around Susie, who sat with Elizabeth's hands resting on her shoulders, and Susanna prayed for a blessed marriage between her daughter and William.

May it be. Susanna cherished the sweet moment with her girls.

Thomas
December 25, 1834
Fairmount, Kentucky

With the birth of each grandchild over the past several years, Thomas had become accustomed to spending time whittling away his nerves. He sat near the hearth, fashioning the wood into a toy chicken. Mary sat opposite him while her husband, Richard, smoked a pipe beside her. Susie's two boys, Francis and Tom—ages three and one—had fallen asleep near Mary, long after Elizabeth and Susanna had left for the Wilcox home to assist Susie in welcoming another child into the world. Mary's three little ones slept in the loft. Although he'd experienced the waiting before, the uncertainty was no less for this one. Would the child be healthy? A boy or a girl? Would his daughter fare well?

What he anticipated more than anything was the delight in Susanna's eyes, which brought as much joy to him as the new child. His wife had been a wonderful mother, yet she flourished as a grandmother. She doted on the grandchildren and helped with household chores until the girls could manage without her, which was always far sooner than Susanna hoped. But even his strong-willed wife knew when to step back and let her daughters take charge of their household.

And William had proved to be a good father. Thomas had been wrong about him, a fact Susanna never let him forget. Susie had married a capable farmer who provided a helping hand to Thomas whenever he needed one. William's peach orchards were a success, and Thomas didn't mind the year-round peach pies and preserves, even if he'd never admit it.

"It's been longer than I expected." Mary yawned and stretched her arms. "Christmas Day come and almost gone. Too bad we couldn't have spent the holiday with Uncle Eli and Aunt Lizzie after they traveled all the way from Louisville. I'm glad Uncle Elias invited them to Christmas dinner, but I would have liked to spend more time with my cousins. What stories they tell of the city."

"Better that they have a merry time than wait on pins and needles with the rest of us." Thomas had welcomed Eli and Lizzie and their brood of nine children. After his sister and brother-in-law moved to Louisville, they didn't often make the thirteen-mile trip to Fairmount.

The door opened, and a windswept Elizabeth stumbled into the cabin.

"Father, you're needed." Elizabeth brushed the stray pieces of hair from her face.

Thomas paused to query Mary with a look. But Elizabeth stepped forward, regaining his attention. "Now, Father."

Mary reached for her sister. "Elizabeth, has the baby come?"

"Mary, please stay with the children."

Thomas rose from the chair as fast as his overworked knees allowed, grabbed a coat, and followed Elizabeth out into the cold.

The pair's quick footsteps on the path to the Wilcox cabin pierced the silent night. When Thomas saw the cabin, he picked up his pace and scurried through the front door.

Inside, the strong bellow of a newborn welcomed them.

"Thank God," Thomas said. "Elizabeth, what . . ."

Mrs. Thixton walked out of the sleeping room with a swaddled, crying bundle. The woman's eyes were tired and red. "Thomas, go on." She directed him into the room with a nod.

Thomas's feet wouldn't move, paralyzed as if he'd ingested the poison hemlock that grew down by the fork. Elizabeth took his arm and guided him into the chamber.

His wife sat in a chair, her body crumpled forward, holding Susie's hand. Thomas moved his gaze to Susie's pale face, then to William, who was crouched on the floor in a corner like a man hiding from a rabid coyote, rocking back and forth. Elizabeth nudged Thomas forward when Susanna sat up and peered at him through a tear-stained face.

"She didn't make it, Thomas," she moaned. "Our baby didn't make it."

Thomas
October 1835
Fairmount, Kentucky

No father should bury his child. In the past ten months since Susie died, Thomas had taken his grief out on his wife, growling at her like a bear disturbed during its hibernation. Today, Susanna finally put him in his place.

When the morning coffee wasn't in its place on the cherry table after he came in from feeding the animals, Thomas muttered an expletive aimed at his wife.

"Thomas, do you really think you're the only one hurting around here?" Susanna pounded a fist on the table. "If you need something to do, go into the fields and work out your anger. Go visit your grandchildren. Little Mary, Tom, and Francis need us more than ever, not to mention William. Do anything. But don't you dare come at me with words like that again."

Thomas had experienced Susanna's ire before. They typically had it out and then moved on. But this time, he held his tongue, left the cabin, and walked down to Floyds Fork. The warm sun and clear sky taunted him, echoing the memory of Susie's blue eyes. He lowered his weary body to a boulder on the banks of the creek under a large oak tree. Its blood-red leaves provided shade from the sun and served as a beautiful yet painful reminder of death. He picked up smooth, small stones and skipped them over the water's surface. The creek's gentle gurgling soothed his soul, though his insides felt raw as the new skin under a blister.

Throughout his life, he'd controlled every situation—the decision to move west, which parcel of land to buy, what crops to plant, when to harvest. Yet in this silence, he realized so much had been out of his control. The babies Susanna had lost. Had she felt this grief with each loss? God forgive him for never asking. He couldn't fix Elizabeth's hurting heart during her first marriage or each of her husbands' deaths. Try as he might, he had been powerless to stop the earth from trembling, a late frost from damaging a crop, or a drought from parching a harvest. Life and death. Growth and harvest. How had he ever believed he had authority over such things?

He felt—rather than heard—the faint words of a Methodist minister come over him like the cool autumn breeze. *I am the vine, ye are the branches: He that abideth in me, and I in him, the same bringeth forth much fruit: for without me ye can do nothing.*

Thomas realized he was powerless. Without God, he was nothing.

A freedom washed over him. He didn't have to dominate his fields. He never could nor would.

Yet he had a decision to make. Could he humble himself and be honest with his wife? Was he willing to both comfort Susanna in her grief and share in it? Dread raised his defenses like a porcupine's quills. However, he was old enough—and hopefully wise enough—to do the right thing.

Thomas stood and shuffled back to the house, opening and closing the door in a way that prevented the hinge from squeaking. He stared at their sleeping chamber where they kept the family chest that had traveled with them from Pennsylvania. With hesitation, Thomas inched into the room. He knelt on one knee with a groan and opened the lid, the musty scent of memories overpowering him. Thomas gently removed the family Bible and carried it to the cherry table. Opening the Bible to the back, he ran a finger along his and Susanna's names and the date of their marriage. Thomas's eyes studied each line, looking at each girl's date of birth. The faded memories both filled and broke his heart.

From the Bible's case, he took the iron gall ink bottle and goose quill. He shook and uncorked the bottle, then carefully dipped the quill into the ink. Next to Susie's name and birth, with a shaky hand, he wrote: "Died December 25, 1834. Beloved daughter." Under his grandsons' names and birthdates, he added, "Mary Wilcox. Born December 25, 1834."

"Thomas?"

He looked up from the Bible as a single tear left a trail of salt down his time- and sun-worn skin. "I'm so sorry, Susanna."

His wife of fifty years hurried to his side and wrapped her arms around him. God willing, he and Susanna would learn to carry this burden together.

Susanna
Spring 1842
Fairmount, Kentucky

Susanna rocked forward and backward, the wooden porch chair groaning with age. Creation sang of spring with its golden forsythia, violet redbuds, and alabaster flowers on the dogwood trees. But the discordant tones in her heart couldn't harmonize with the beauty surrounding her.

Of all the years she and Thomas had been together, the six years since Susie's death had been the sweetest. Or maybe bittersweet more aptly described those years. Susanna had watched Thomas relish the days he spent with William and the grandchildren. He was especially smitten by little Mary who'd sit in his lap, listening to stories of days gone by. Thomas hired local hands to work the fields, passing along his knowledge of tilling, planting, and harvesting.

Thomas had changed that October day six years ago. He never told her what happened down by the river, but he'd been transformed. She sensed he no longer carried the burden of responsibility. He stood taller, his eyes shone brighter, and he laughed more heartily. God seemed to have given her a better, more genuine version of her husband. However, grief still weighed down a corner of their hearts.

Now, she carried a double portion of heartache with his passing. It'd been six months since he'd been buried under the sugar maple tree at the age of seventy-five. She shouldn't complain. Susanna had had fifty-seven good years with Thomas. Hard years. Happy times. Tough days. But filled with enough memories to last the next twenty years if the good Lord pleased to keep her on this earth that long. And Susanna hoped to use her time wisely and pass down to her children and grandchildren the faith, hope, and love she and Thomas had shared.

Susanna rose from the rocker and walked inside the cabin. The Bible lay on the table where she had left it. Throughout the winter months, the darkness and loneliness oppressed her too heavily to record the loss on paper. Susanna turned to the page where her father had written their names, births, and the date of their wedding many years ago. She picked up the quill, dipped it in the ink bottle, and wrote beside Thomas's name and birthdate: "Died October 19, 1841. May his legacy live on."

Part 2

MARY WILCOX

Mary Wilcox
December 25, 1841
Fairmount, Kentucky

I killed my mama seven years ago. No one ever told me I killed her, but she died bringing me into this world, so I reckon that counts. Pa seems to have forgotten my mama since he went quick and married Miss Nancy when I was three. I guess he figured Francis, Tom, and me needed a ma. But Nancy ain't my mama. She and my pa have Sarah Ellen now. She's just a wee babe. I help with Sarah Ellen when she's fussing. Most of the time, I try to be real good.

Aunt Elizabeth tells me my mama was as pretty as sunshine on a spring day. Even her name Susanna is pretty, don't you think? Too bad I don't look like her with my mud-colored hair and eyes. Sometimes, I can't help but think of her, like this morning when Aunt Elizabeth wanted me to put on my best dress for Christmas. I put up a fuss. How can I think of such things when today is the day my mama died? I'm sorry, Baby

Jesus, for being ugly to Auntie. But I don't want to celebrate your birthday. Or mine. I want my mama.

Sitting in front of the big fireplace on cold winter days feels like a warm hug. Winter in Kentucky isn't as bad as Pennsylvania. At least that's what Grandmother tells me. I don't even mind fixing supper with Nancy on these cold days on account of the fire. Truth told, in the cold months, I want to stay inside. Except when Sarah Ellen is squawking. Then I'll go to Grandmother and Grandfather Graham's house.

Grandfather built that log house way back when he first came to Kentucky some forty years ago. It has two levels and a smooth wood floor. I imagine the warmth of Mama's feet climbing up and down the loft ladder, almost like she's still there. Grandfather told me stories about the days when this area was barely settled. He was still working in the orchard with Pa and the boys until he died in October. I sure do miss him.

Aunt Elizabeth tells me Grandmother is a tough old bird. I'm not quite sure what she means, but Grandfather said she learned to be a strong woman living on the frontier for forty years. My mama was named after her mama, so they are both called Susanna. But if my mama was as pretty as spring sunshine, I'd say Grandmother is as bold as the colors on an autumn day. Her deep red hair is streaked with silver. She's mighty beautiful to me.

Pa built our house just before he and Mama got married. He says the neighbors—the Thixtons, the Hayses, and the Welshes—all helped to build the house. The boys and me, we sleep in the loft. Pa and Nancy, and now Sarah Ellen, sleep downstairs in the sleeping room.

In the winter months, I dream of playing outside in the summer sun with my brothers. I don't know what most brothers are like, but Tom and Francis seem to tolerate me good enough. Tom is one year older than me. Francis is two years older than him. Last summer they taught me how to catch crawfish down at Big Run. That was fine, but I prefer picking the wild berries that grow near Big Run. The strawberries, bright red and juicy in summertime, and blackberries as big as my thumb in the fall, grow wild all over our land.

Tom and Francis are old enough to help Pa with the orchard. They're learning how to prune the peach trees in the spring and shape them so the sunshine is caught up in their leaves. In the summer, mice and squirrels and deer try to steal those peaches. Pa and the boys kept busy last summer fighting them and the other pests. All fall, Aunt Elizabeth, Nancy, Grandmother, and me, we picked peaches, we washed peaches, we cooked peaches, and we ate peach preserves, peach pie, and peach cobbler. Pa takes the peaches to Louisville with his gray mare and wagon to get the best price. Some of our peaches even end up all the way down in New Orleans by a steamboat on the Ohio River. Imagine that.

Now that I'm getting grown up, this year I get to help with the chickens and the milk cow. One day, I hope we have a whole farm full of strawberries and blackberries. Grandmother says my mama liked strawberries when she was my age. I think growing strawberries would make my mama proud.

JENNY SMITH

November 6, 1843

I put my pinky finger next to the branch and compare the two. The wood is smaller than my finger, so I cut the branch from the limb with a knife. In one month, I'll be nine years old, and that makes me old enough to help Pa and my brothers prune the peach trees. We just had the first frost, and I'm remembering all that Pa has taught me. The scrawny branches won't bear good fruit. But the red branches, the ones bigger than my little finger, they are the ones I want to keep for next year's crop. Pa says that peaches need to breathe lots of air and feel the sun. Peaches sound a lot like me.

The day is cool, and I hear the rustling of the fall leaves as a cool breeze blows hair into my face. The sun shines bright in the sky, enough that despite the chill in the air, I wipe sweat from my brow with my forearm. I take a look at another branch, but I think it might be diseased. I turn around to ask Pa. I see him sitting with his back against a tree. I skip over to him, guessing he's eating the piece of cheese Nancy gave him before we left the house.

"Pa . . . ?" I study his face. He's not eating. My stomach doesn't rumble with hunger but with fear. "Pa, are you okay?"

"I'm fine. Just needed a rest." He tries to laugh but coughs instead. "Your pa isn't as young as he used to be." He tries to take in a deep breath but clutches one hand against his chest. He looks as white as cotton on a cottonwood tree. This ain't like my pa. My hands begin to quiver like leaves blowing in a storm. I don't know what to do.

"Tom? Francis?" I shout, frantically searching the orchard for my brothers. I find them, dig my feet into the grass, and run as fast as I can. Breathless, I tug at Francis's sleeve and pull him.

"What're you doing, Mary?" He shoos me away like I'm a fly. "We don't have time for play."

"I'm not playing. Something's wrong with Pa." I look into my brother's eyes, but all I see is doubt. I know I've told fibs, but I'm not fibbing now. He's got to believe me. "Come on, Francis!" My pleading convinces him, and he yells for Tom. Both boys follow me to the tree where Pa is resting.

The three of us gather around Pa. I look at Tom, then Francis. I lift my eyebrows and purse my lips in a way that says *I told you so*.

"Boys, help me up and let's go to the cabin." He tries to stand up, but his legs collapse under him.

Francis and Tom each wrap an arm around Pa's back and get him on his feet. Pa keeps an arm around each of their necks, walking slowly. But I can tell Francis and Tom are carrying a heavy load.

I run ahead of them to the cabin, open the door, and run through it. A few dry leaves follow me into the cabin.

"Mary, close the door, you're letting in the insects." Nancy is always fussing at me for leaving the door open, but I don't close it. "Pa's dying." I don't know what else to say.

Nancy stares at me, then dashes to the door and pales as she moves out of the way and watches Tom and Francis help Pa into a chair.

"William, what's wrong?" Nancy kneels in front of her husband, wiping away the sweat glistening on his forehead.

"I'm just a bit tired. Nothing to concern yourself over." He pats Nancy's hand that rests on his knee.

"I'll make you some lemon balm and peppermint tea." Nancy stands but doesn't head toward the kitchen. I overhear her whisper to Tom to ride Pa's horse to Glen Hope where Dr. Johnston lives.

I scamper up the ladder to the loft and grab my ragdoll, Dora, that Aunt Elizabeth made me. I hide upstairs for a few minutes, hugging Dora, my companion. A tear slides down my face, but something tells me there's no time for tears, so I return to Pa's side, ragdoll in tow.

Finally, I hear the hoofbeats of two horses. While Nancy continues to encourage Pa to drink the tea, I run to the door and open it, Sarah Ellen on my heels. I return to Pa's side, but by the time Doc walks through the door, I can see Pa is halfway to heaven.

"You'll be okay, Pa." I say these words because I need to believe they are true.

March 1850

The rooster crows loudly, and I open my eyes enough to see the sun just starting to peek through the windows. Reality hits me like a splash of cold water on a winter's day when I remember that Pa is dead. Even though it's been seven years, the truth still jars me. I put on my corset and petticoats over my chemise before pulling on my dress. The fire is almost out, so I toss a few logs into the fireplace to take the chill out of the air. Aunt Elizabeth, who moved in with us after Pa died, is already up spending her time with God. She says she needs the good Lord's strength to make it through the day. After the past few years, I'd say we all do. But I'm not sure the God who takes and takes and takes is worth asking for anything.

After Pa died, we buried him next to Mama in the family cemetery back in the fields, surrounded by big oak and sugar maple trees. Sometimes I go talk to him and Mama, just like we're having a conversation over supper. I tell them how I started my strawberry patch and that I pick the plump wild blackberries out near Big Run in the fall to make ends meet.

This morning, I make coffee over the fire, and Aunt Elizabeth puts out bread and cheese and cold meat for breakfast.

"Tom, come get your food. It's time to get working," I yell up to the loft.

Tom is the man of the house now, working the land. Francis followed through on Pa's dying wish that he'd learn a trade and apprenticed with a blacksmith, Mr. Sanderson, Aunt Elizabeth's relation by her second marriage. Francis lives at Mrs. Mary Ann Howorth's boarding house in Louisville. He says the food is decent and the pay is good enough to keep us fed, but I sure wish he'd come back home. I've visited him two times. Louisville has as many people as an anthill, everybody scurrying here and there. The air is heavy with coal soot and smells of sewage. It's a nasty place, if you ask me. I prefer marveling at the rolling hills that go on for miles, breathing in the air scented with honeysuckle, and listening to the leaves rustling on the trees.

In Pa's will, he made sure one-third of our land went to his widow. Wouldn't you know, Nancy married Mr. John Thornsberry four months after Pa died, and she and Sarah Ellen moved to Louisville. Mr. Thornsberry died this winter, so my guess is Nancy is looking for another husband to wed.

All that leaves Tom to look after the peach orchard. Mr. Thixton and George Welsh, Francis's friend, come and help Thomas since he's still learning.

"Mary," Aunt Elizabeth interrupts my string of thoughts. "We're running low on flour and cornmeal. Will you go over to Mr. Wiggington's store today?"

"Mind if I go to Mr. Hays's store? I'll stop by Grandmother's on my way home." I turn my back and look out the window at the blue sky so Aunt Elizabeth can't see that I am passing a white lie. It's true that a long walk on a spring day in Kentucky shouldn't be passed up. But neither do I want to miss the chance to run into George Welsh at the store.

Tom finally meanders down the ladder from the loft and sits down, gobbling everything in front of him. He looks like a man now with his broad shoulders and stands taller than Pa ever did. He has Mama's cornhusk-colored hair and eyes as bright as a bluebird. I caught Martha Thixton making eyes at him during church last week, so I know the girls think he's handsome.

Soon Tom is out the door to start a long day of working in the orchard. After cleaning up breakfast with Aunt Elizabeth, I grab my bonnet and wrap a shawl around my shoulders to keep the chill off.

I walk to Bardstown Turnpike and turn south toward the store. The turnpike, nothing but a buffalo trace when Grandfather moved here, had been widened to sixty feet and covered with macadamized limestone a few years after I was born to make travel easy from Bardstown to Louisville. Houses and businesses line the turnpike for several miles—from Fern Creek, the area three miles north of here, to the covered bridge of Floyds Fork and its toll house—and give the area its nickname, Stringtown.

As I walk along the road, I see the tree buds and grass are just beginning to show their bright spring green. In a few more weeks, the land will be in full bloom, showcasing fields and orchards bursting with color. I love spring because of the promise of new life. Spring gives me hope for the things to come. But this time of year also promises thunderstorms and rain. Never know what weather you'll get from a Kentucky day—or apparently, me. More than once, Aunt Elizabeth has told me my mood changes as fast as the spring weather. Bright and sunny one moment, stormy and ready to destroy you the next.

As I near the store, which also serves as the local post office, I fluff the bow on my bonnet. I open the door, and a bell rings announcing my presence.

Mr. Hays comes out to greet me. "What can I do you for, Mary?"

"I'd like some wheat flour and cornmeal, please, Mr. Hays." My eyes dart around the small store and land on George Welsh. My stomach buzzes like the hornet nest Tom stirred up by accident last summer. I glance down, pretending I don't see him, while I wait for Mr. Hays.

"Mary," George calls my name. "What are doing all the way down here today?"

I fear my cheeks are turning the color of my best strawberries. "I'm checking on my grandmother on my way home. It's such a nice day that I didn't mind the extra distance."

I look back to Mr. Hays, who has prepared the flour and meal. He gives me a quick wink. "George, why don't you be a gentleman and help Mary carry this back to the house."

Oh, heavens. Mr. Hays is always putting his nose in people's business.

"My pleasure, Mr. Hays. I need to check in with Tom, so I was headed that way myself." George hefts the flour, holds open the door, and gestures for me to proceed.

I exit the store, and then George and I fall into comfortable conversation on the way to Grandmother's. We chat about the responsibilities of spring—for me, cutting runners from the strawberry plants and fertilizing them to ensure a better harvest this year. I've become known for my sweet berries that flourish in a garden I'd begun several years ago. I sell my strawberry jam, syrup, and vinegar throughout the area. I'm quite proud of what I've accomplished and think Mama would be too.

George said he'll start pruning the apple and pear trees on his father's land, while also helping Tom when he can. Francis and George were particular friends before Francis was apprenticed. George visits Francis every few months in Louisville and carries gifts of his favorite food from me and Aunt Elizabeth.

Soon enough, we are at my grandmother's house. I thank George for his company and turn to go up the steps to the house, wishing work could wait and spring would last longer.

Grandmother, now eighty-three years old, still lives in the house my grandfather built. Since his death a few years before Pa, Aunt Elizabeth and I make a point to visit nearly every day. While Grandmother has a hard time walking the mile to our house, she gets along fine on her own. She still keeps a garden and has a few cats, which she allows inside when the weather gets dreadfully cold. She says she doesn't like those cats—only feels sorry for them. But I know better. Behind that tough exterior, she's as soft as a kitten's fur.

"Well, why are you here so early today?" Grandmother slowly leans forward in her rocking chair and uses her strong arms to help straighten her legs into a standing position. "These old bones don't work too well in the cold weather, but I got to thank God Almighty I'm still here to complain about it."

"We're all glad you're still here." I lean over and peck her on the cheek. "What can I help you with today?"

After chatting, helping Grandmother gather firewood, and mending a few pieces of clothing, I'm on my way back to the house and ponder how my grandmother has lived through so many changes. She was married in Pennsylvania and helped Grandfather clear and settle this piece of land in Kentucky. She had three daughters and lost my mama and her husband. Grandmother is approaching an age where I fear I'll lose her soon. In some ways, I feel I am just beginning my life while hers is coming to an end. But both of us hold on to hope. Me, I'm hoping for a future with a family of my own. One yet to be seen. I think Grandmother is waiting for the same thing: a reunion with a daughter and beloved husband.

June 1859

I stand in the middle of the strawberry patch wiping sweat from my brow while I look upon a flurry of five-petaled white flowers. Any day now, the crimson gems will begin to develop and mature. Each year I learn a bit more. To fertilize in the spring, make sure to water if summer rains are sparse, and share the plentiful harvest with friends and neighbors.

"Mama," my son calls, snatching me out of my reverie. Hearing myself called Mama is the sweetest sound I can ever imagine.

"I'm coming, dear." I pick up the hem of my dress and traipse gently between the strawberry bushes until I reach

Hillaire, who sits in the grass with his arms reaching for me to pick him up.

"Mama, look!" he says with a newfound appreciation of words, showing me the petal of a strawberry blossom. Hillaire has filled the past months with both joy and hardship, sleepless nights and sweet cuddles during afternoon naps. He was unexpected. This life is unexpected. And yet, I think that's exactly what has made him such a blessing.

One year ago, my scoundrel of a distant cousin, Richard, appeared at our house with a young girl holding an infant. We soon learned they weren't married, and the girl couldn't care for the baby. Even worse, Richard refused to take responsibility for both the girl and child.

My dream of marriage had yet to happen. At twenty-three, I wasn't yet a spinster, but George had married a lovely girl four years earlier, and with that, my heart had been wounded yet again. Not that George and I had ever developed anything more than a friendship, although perhaps that friendship was a bit dearer on my side than his.

Aunt Elizabeth and I briefly discussed the girl and her baby. In her wisdom, Aunt said this was a decision that only God could give me direction on. She invited the young mother in, and she shooed Richard out to Thixton's tavern across the pike. "Go walk down by the creek. You can always hear God's voice better out there." Oh, how well she knew me.

By the time I reached Big Run, I had thought through all the reasons taking an infant was foolish. Elizabeth was sixty-eight. While Francis still brought in an income as a blacksmith, Tom was not yet married, and I still helped him in the orchards during harvest. How could I raise a child?

The banks of Big Run were full, thanks to a recent summer storm. The creek resounded like the wings of a thousand cherubs in front of God's throne. Like Moses's burning bush, this was my holy ground.

"What do I do?" I whispered to no one, yet cried out to God. And in that moment, I knew.

For the next several months, we housed the young girl so she could feed the baby until he could take condensed milk in place of his mother's milk. Mr. Borden's new creation promised to be safer than cow's milk and just as good for the baby. Thankfully, we could easily purchase it from the nearby store. We sent off the poor girl with enough money for a few months. I know little of Miss Rousseau, other than she went back to Louisville.

Hillaire quickly became a beloved member of our family. Tom dotes on him like any good uncle should, tossing him in the air, which produces giggles from deep within Hillaire's belly, leaving all of us laughing. Aunt Elizabeth is as proud as my mama would have been of a grandson. She sews him clothing and created a beautiful patchwork quilt for cold winter nights. Francis now lives two miles away from us in Cedar Creek and works for Mr. Nutter. He made a beautiful brass and wood baby rattle that entertains Hillaire for hours. Until her death, Grandmother bragged about her great-grandson any time she had an ear to listen.

Not that people aren't talking. More than once I've stumbled upon conversations between two or three neighborhood ninnies discussing Hillaire's less-than-honorable origins, as well as my chances of any man ever marrying me. I'm ashamed to admit that these comments sting like a bee that leaves a welt throbbing with every heartbeat. How can a child control the circumstances under which he is conceived? And if a man doesn't care for me enough to take on my child, then he isn't a man I want to marry. If they have nothing better to talk about, let them chatter.

Amid my joy of becoming a mother—for I truly accept Hillaire as my very own—fourteen months later, loss shattered our family yet again. While her death was not unexpected, my grandmother suffered from apoplexy that left her partially paralyzed and unable to care for herself. This strong-willed woman I'd always esteemed had lost her will to live but not to fight. We moved her into our house—quite against her will—so Aunt Elizabeth and I could care for her. And just a month later, Grandmother passed from this world filled with death and sorrow to one with a promise of no more pain and tears.

Though it has taken time to learn how to raise a child while maintaining the responsibilities of the orchard, I manage. Hillaire may not have come from my womb, but he is embedded in my heart as deeply as the peach trees are in our orchard.

December 1861

In a few years' time, a series of events has occurred that I can't comprehend how I survived—other than by my love for Hillaire.

Aunt Elizabeth, at the age of seventy-one, left us. I'd assumed, like Grandmother, she'd live into her eighties. Almost two years later, her absence is palpable in every nook and cranny of this house. I had hoped to protect Hillaire from the grief of this world, but I was weak as a split rail fence rotted through and through. Aunt's love, wisdom, and support had been the one constant—the only constant—in my life. Although I never told her, she was a mother to me. I don't think I appreciated that until she was gone. Unlike my parents, she is buried with her Sanderson relatives at Cave Hill Cemetery in Louisville. How I wish she was in the family cemetery where I could talk with her when I need her wisdom.

Yet sorrow upon sorrow plagues our dwindling family as Francis has also died. On his recent trip to Louisville, he fell sick from the putrid air and shallow wells of the city. He died on April 30, and we returned Francis to his rightful home next to Mama and Pa.

Francis willed Tom three-quarters of the land, while I received one-fourth and cash notes. Dear Francis hadn't forgotten Sarah Ellen after all these years and left her ten dollars. But Francis made George Welsh trustee of Tom's portion of the inheritance. Considering Tom had sold Francis his share of the land in 1858 for $1000, his inheritance is significant. So why did Francis want George to act as Tom's trustee? I have no answers. Neither will Tom—nor George—give me any.

Of course, I'm not naive. While Tom continues to live with us and work the orchard, he spends most evenings late into the night at Thixton's tavern. Although I've had my concerns, I've never considered anything untoward was going on. Now, I suspect more than country gossip is happening at the tavern for Francis to limit Tom's access to his inheritance.

Since George is the executor of Francis's will, he is helping us make the difficult decision to sell five hundred and twelve acres to Mr. Ash, who has also purchased the two hundred and twelve acres that belonged to Aunt Elizabeth. Mr. Ash has been kind enough to tell me I am welcome to walk along Big Run. And he added, "Hillaire too. Boys need a creek to play and fish in."

We have not protected Grandfather Graham's legacy. The land that he loved so much is slowly being sold.

For the past several months, all the conversations in the stores, taverns, and church gatherings have rumbled of possible war. Kentucky voted to remain neutral, which seems like a feeble-minded gesture to me. In our area of Jefferson County, few families own slaves, but with most farms in the state producing tobacco, hemp, corn, and flax, many Kentuckians sympathize with the South and want things to stay the way they've always been.

And today, Tom and George enlisted in the Union Army.

I am alone on the orchard with a three-year-old son.

I wish I had Aunt Elizabeth's faith. I can hear her telling me that weeping may remain for the night but joy comes in the morning. But she's not here to assure me of that eternal promise.

December 1864

Thank God for neighbors. Over the past several years, Thomas Thixton, a farmer and the tavern owner, and his wife, Rebecca, have stopped by often and lent a hand as needed. When Hillaire turned six this year, Mr. Wiggington offered to allow him to restock the shelves and interact with the customers at the store just across Bardstown Turnpike. Hillaire enjoys his days with Mr. Wiggington, and I spend my time tending to the orchard and berries, as well as the chickens for eggs and the cow for milk and butter. With these basics, we survive.

"Open the damn door!"

I awake to banging on the door on a cold December night. The voice isn't familiar, and while I nearly jump out of bed, I go straight to Hillaire's bed and wrap my arms around him. "Shhh. Let's pretend we're not here," I whisper while I sit down on the bed and hold him in my lap. I grab the quilt Aunt Elizabeth made for Hillaire and put it around us, enfolding us in her love.

The banging continues, and I hear the men try to force open the door. "We ain't playing around. Open up the door." Multiple men's voices shout in agreement.

Over the past three years, our area has had a few exchanges with Union and Confederate soldiers. And our orchard has paid a toll of their passage through the area, feeding both Cavalry horses and soldiers alike. On one occasion, five hundred Confederates attacked the Indiana Cavalry just miles from us in Oakdale, across from what was Colonel George Hancock's property. The gossip in the area whispered that the Southern Cavalry hid in the ravine on Mr. Hancock's land. After all, he owned twenty-two slaves at the beginning of the war.

But these are no soldiers at the door. Threats to take our valuables course through the door.

We've heard the rumors about gangs roaming the countryside. The blood in my veins runs as cold as Big Run in the winter when I think about what they might do to me or Hillaire. Maybe they've had too much to drink and won't see the smoke coming from the chimney. I decide to take a chance and wait them out while I pray for God's protection over us.

Finally, the men's voices fade into the distance, and I lie down in Hillaire's bed and pull the blankets over both of us. Morning can't come soon enough.

Within minutes, Hillaire's breathing becomes deep and regular, but my mind runs wild with a thousand questions. What if the men come back? Who are they? Are others in danger?

When the sun finally starts to rise, I climb out of bed to make a fire and some coffee. Strong coffee after a sleepless night.

A knock on the door causes me to gasp and drop a mug.

"Mary, it's Thomas Thixton. I'm checking on you and the boy."

I let out a sigh, not realizing I've been holding my breath. I walk to the door and hastily unlock the bolt that had protected us hours before.

"Mr. Thixton!" I gesture for him to enter in from the cold. His father, William, helped Pa build this house before my parents married. "Did those rabble-rousers bother you and Rebecca last night?"

"I fired a few rounds and scared them off. But others weren't so lucky." He shakes his head in regret. "They started at Hays Spring and made it all the way up the pikeway near the Hikes family. Mr. Carrithers's horse was stolen. Mr. Curry had $600 pilfered, and they took his grandfather's watch to boot. One man was treating Mrs. Kalfus improperly, if you catch my drift, while another robbed her husband at gunpoint. When Mr. Kalfus came to his wife's aid, they shot him dead."

"Oh, my," I gasp.

"Mary, I don't know what you did last night, but I sure am glad you and the boy are here this morning." Mr. Thixton pats me on my shoulder as my brothers would have. I fix him coffee while he sits near the hearth. When he empties his cup, we exchange final pleasantries, and he leaves to check on other families.

After an idle morning, I bundle myself and Hillaire into layers to protect us from the cold. I hold Hillaire's hand as we cross Bardstown Turnpike to Mr. Wiggington's store in need of coffee. He greets me, but his haggard face tells me that he, too, was awake much of the night.

"Mary, I don't know what this world is coming to." He rubs his hand through his beard in thought and thumbs through a newspaper. "Rumor has it these miscreants are known for killing, thieving, and looting. According to Mr. Prentice, the editor of the *Louisville Daily Journal*, their leader is not a man but a woman named Sue Mundy."

"A woman?" I question Mr. Wiggington's story, wondering what kind of woman would dare to lead a group of delinquents.

"Yes, ma'am. She wears men's clothing and lets her long dark hair flow loose as she rides her horse—not sidesaddle, mind you." He shakes his head at the scandalous gossip. "But others say Mr. Prentice invents it all just to sell more newspapers."

I hold Hillaire a bit closer to me. Whether these scoundrels are led by a man or a woman, I breathe a sigh of relief that I didn't find out.

My body shivers under my threadbare wool coat as I enter Mr. Hays's store, which also serves as the Fairmount Post Office. Though I can't afford to buy much, I continue my weekly visit in hopes of a letter from the post. The door jingles as welcomingly as it did when I was fifteen, yet it only reminds me of easier, happier times.

"Mary," Mr. Hays greets me with unexpected enthusiasm. "You have a letter. I believe it's from Tom." He finds the letter and walks around the counter to hold it out in front of me. "Soldier's Letter" is printed on the outside of the envelope. I stand frozen in fear, unwilling to accept the letter from him. With a sigh of apprehension, I pull at the tip of each of my gloved fingers, taking off the glove on my left hand, then my right, and place the gloves on the counter. I reach into my skirt pocket and hand two coins to Mr. Hays for the postage I owe as the recipient of the letter. With shaking hands—maybe from the cold, maybe from fear—I accept the envelope. I gently open it, pull out the letter, and unfold the paper. My eyes glide over Tom's familiar handwriting. He is mustering out of the 11th Infantry, Company H, and will be home by Christmas.

Not one to easily cry, I can't help but look at Mr. Hays with tears in my eyes. "Finally, a Christmas worth celebrating!"

Mr. Hays steps forward and takes my hands in his. "Mary, you've done a right good job these past years keeping the orchard going and raising a son. You deserve to celebrate."

"Thank you, Mr. Hays. I think we do. We all do."

I hear the door open as I busy myself cooking over the fireplace. Some things never change. I still prefer to be in front of the fire than outside on a cold winter's day. "Hillaire?" I ask.

"It's me, Mary."

Without even a knock, Tom enters the door as if he'd just left hours—not years—before.

"Tom!" I toss the handling rag on the table and run and throw my arms around him, ensuring this moment is not my imagination. "You're home." He wraps me into his arms as tight as ivy around a tree trunk.

"Uncle Tom, you're back!" Hillaire runs to Tom who kneels and grasps Hillaire's shoulders to keep him at arm's length to take in his nephew. "My how you've grown." Tom embraces him and sobs, a deep, heart-wrenching sound.

Hillaire looks at me with concern in his eyes. "Uncle Tom, what's wrong? Aren't you happy to be home?"

"Yes, my boy. I'm happy to be home." He stands and wipes away his tears while my eyes appraise his tall, lanky frame.

I wasn't prepared for the changes I see in my brother. His once broad, strong shoulders stoop as if he is carrying two turnpike milestones on his back. His bright eyes are now darker, the color of storm clouds on the horizon. What have those eyes seen?

We celebrate Christmas—and my birthday. We have little, but with several families joining together, we share in a feast that we haven't enjoyed in years.

JENNY SMITH

October 1865

Tom never really came back to us. Over the past year, he has sold sixty-two acres to John Brown and fifteen acres to Mr. Ash. Tom continues to work the seventeen acres I inherited from Francis, but I can tell his heart is no longer in the work. Though blood still courses through his veins, the brother I once knew bled out on the battlefield.

So I'm not surprised today when Tom tells me he's going west. I let him go with my blessing. He needs to heal, if that is even possible.

"Don't forget us," I plead with him.

"I could never forget," he promises.

His leaving—yet again—creates a deep wound. Time will allow that wound to heal, but I won't deny that I wish I had my brother instead of his promised letters.

January 1873

Winter is the season for death and dying. It is the season I find myself in.

It began three years ago. The signs are easy to recognize in retrospect, but I didn't think much of them at the beginning. When I worked in the orchard or tended to the strawberries, my chest pained me. My breath came short. Sometimes a cough plagued me. But for the most part, my body was strong and healthy. More importantly, life flowed along contentedly like water in a creek bed, moving towards its ultimate purpose while nourishing those it passes along the way.

After the war ended, I enrolled Hillaire in Fairmount School across the street from the old Hancock property, now owned by Mr. Long. Mr. Wiggington, the owner of the general store, had encouraged me to have him schooled rather than stay in the fields. Hillaire was a quick learner and had a knack for business. Mr. Wiggington said, "That boy can sell a rock to the stingiest of my customers."

Sure enough, Hillaire beamed each day when he returned from his mile-long walk from school. While we finished working in the orchard together, he'd chatter about mathematics, history, and geography.

Then the night sweats started. I'd wake up in a fit of coughing, drenched in perspiration. The corset I wore became loose around my abdomen, with no flesh to mold into a comely figure. Three months ago, I found blood on my pillow after a restless night of sleep. I could deny it no longer. I had consumption.

I know what awaits me. Death isn't what I fear. It's the dying. It's leaving Hillaire as my mama left me.

I have spoken to Thomas Thixton. He has agreed to be Hillaire's guardian when I pass. At just fourteen, Hillaire will have a good man to guide him into adulthood. I've provided for Hillaire's future—not that money can replace a mother's love. Mr. Thixton, also the executor of my last will and testament, knows my wish is to sell the land to the highest bidder. He is to use the proceeds to see to Hillaire's education, that he works and makes a living, and stays out of bad company. My final desire is for my body to be laid in the cemetery under the old oak and sugar maple trees alongside my family.

Sometimes it seems all I've known is death and loss. Yet I've seen life in all of its seasons. The newness of spring, the growth of summer, the harvest of fall, and the cessation of activity that comes with winter.

I've learned the seasons of life are all beautiful in their own way even when tinged with loss and sorrow. I pray Hillaire grows old enough to see all the seasons in his life, his children's lives, and his grandchildren's lives. With this, my life will have had meaning and purpose. And I think my mama would be proud.

Part 3

ROBERT HILLAIRE WILCOX

Robert Hillaire Wilcox Journal
July 17, 1879
Fairmount, Kentucky

Yesterday, I turned twenty-one, of legal age, and everything I have known is about to change. Early this morning, Mr. Thixton and I left at sunrise to take the wagon north on Bardstown Turnpike to Louisville. The day was clear and hot as Hades, even in the early morning. During the two-hour trip, we discussed the weather's impact on the summer crops, then mellowed into comfortable silence, the dust and crunching of the horses' hooves on the macadamized road filling the air.

When we arrived at the Jefferson County Courthouse, we left the horses and wagon at a nearby stable to be cared for before the trip home. As I approached the courthouse, its imposing four limestone columns and Greek Revival architecture were only a small portion of what had my stomach tied in knots. We made our way up the steps and to the office of Mr. English, the commissioner who settled my guardianship account. Mr. Thixton and I both signed the agreement that determined I am to receive $364.

For the past six years, Mr. Thixton has been a fair guardian and has justly managed the $800 from the sale of Mother's land. He paid for the education I craved at Morrison Academy. Yet Mr. Thixton wisely would not give in when, as a sixteen-year-old boy, I begged for a horse to ride to and from school and my work at the general store. "All of my children walked to school, and you will be no different." His words echo in my ears, not with bitterness, but with gratefulness that I was treated no differently than his children.

The Thixtons already had six mouths to feed when I joined their family. Will, the oldest Thixton boy and my closest friend since I can remember, made room for me in his small sleeping room alongside his younger brother. Neither Mr. nor Mrs. Thixton ever made me feel like a burden.

Even as she lay dying, my mother was preparing for my future and arranged for Mr. Thixton to be my guardian after her too-early death. Honestly, who else would have taken me in? Certainly not Richard H. Wilcox, my father, a shallow, irresponsible man. He willingly relinquished any responsibility for me and the woman who birthed me when I was an infant. I shiver at the thought of what life would have been like with that man. I still can't shake the memory of when he dared to show his face at the public auction when the last seventeen acres of Wilcox and Graham land were sold to Dr. A. R. Groves. I hate to think the worst of people, but I fear his greed and years of bad decisions clouded his judgment, and he believed the courts would grant him guardianship of me—and the money. He was absent from my life except when he showed up at our house, inebriated and smelling of alcohol and vomit, begging Mother for a loan. She knew better than to oblige him.

Mother, I know you can't read this journal, but I write with the hope that you somehow know how grateful I am for you, and I will prove myself worthy of all you gave me.

Jefferson County Settlement Books, page 46
July 17, 1879
Louisville, Kentucky

> Thomas H. Thixton Guardian Account Payable with his ward R. H. Wilcox. Balance due ward $364.90.
>
> Rec'd of my Guardian Thos H Thixton the above balance of three hundred and sixty-four and 90/100 dollars in full of all monies and other property coming me. I being now of full and lawful age twenty-one years. I have examined the above account and find it cleared.
> – Hillaire Wilcox
>
> State of Kentucky, Jefferson County, S.E. English, Commissioner

Robert Hillaire Wilcox Journal
July 18, 1879
Fairmount, Kentucky

As I write this, I sit next to what the locals call Fairmount Falls on the Thixton property, about a mile from the house. I come here when I need to think. I like to wander the creek, picking up limestone arrowheads that belonged to the Shawnee who inhabited the land before the white settlers pushed them west.

I am on my own, and that thought weighs on me as heavily as the summer humidity. Sitting beside the waterfall, Floyds Fork cascades into a crystal blue pool at the base of the falls and sings to me. Creation speaks aloud, but it mostly tells how small and insignificant I am. The pounding water, the twittering of birds, and the rhythmic drone of the cicadas reveal that this is not my home. Yet, it is all I know. It's not a real home with parents, siblings, grandparents, and flocks of cousins.

Maybe it's time I live an adventure like one of my fictional heroes, Pierre Aronnax of *Twenty Thousand Leagues under the Seas*. Or maybe my tale is more similar to *The Swiss Family Robinson* since I must build a life from nothing. Years ago, I purchased these books with my meager income from the store, and I've read them until the corners of the pages are as wrinkled as a cox's comb. My inheritance—as much as I make in a year at the general store as a clerk—gives me options, but not peace. Not family. Not a home.

I am no longer a ward of Thomas Thixton. It is time I plan for my future. I have an opportunity to travel to the unknown and write my own story. My hands tremble at the unknown, but my heart also beats with excitement.

The Courier-Journal
Louisville, Kentucky
September 21, 1879

> WANTED—SITUATION—A gentleman aged 21, without family, able to furnish abundant references as to character and capacity, desires a situation as clerk or traveling salesman with a wholesale house. Have years of experience in goods and sales. Knowledgeable

in balancing books. Address H. Wilcox. Fairmount Post Office.

Robert Hillaire Wilcox Journal
December 1, 1879
On the Missouri Pacific Railway

A position awaits me in Kansas City.

Yesterday morning, Will was a good friend and conveyed me and my belongings in the family wagon to Louisville's L&N train station. The cold, damp weather made for a bone-chilling ride, close to three hours long. Yet our conversation was warm, as we retold childhood stories with fond memories.

What preceded my departure was many a goodbye. Mrs. Thixton made me promise I would write, and often. She packed enough food for three days to ensure I wouldn't miss a home-cooked meal. In the weeks leading up to my departure, I went to a tailor who made me proper clothing for a businessman. Will told me that even if I didn't feel the part, I needed to look it. I stayed through the end of November to help the family finish the harvest season, then we celebrated with a grand feast on Thanksgiving Day.

Before yesterday, I had never been on a train. I am sorry to say that the accounts I've read of train travel have been romanticized. A layer of dust, dirt, and soot covers every surface. The temperature varies from sweltering hot to bone-chilling cold when a passenger opens a window to cool the car or rid it of its stale smell. My body aches from the extended time in my second-class seat, and my neck is sore from dozing off in an odd position.

I am thankful the tailor recommended a dark wool sack suit. The loose-fitting jacket keeps me warm in the train car, warmed by only a pot-bellied stove that spews ash into the air. I switched trains in Evansville, arrived in St. Louis this morning, and by evening, I will be in Kansas City, no longer a frontier city with its population of fifty-five thousand.

My adventure has begun, although I do not know what awaits me.

Letter to Mrs. Thixton from Robert H. Wilcox
September 19, 1880
Kansas City, Missouri

Dear Mrs. Thixton,

I received your letter with great joy. You remembered my birthday when no one in this city was even aware of my existence. To know that someone, somewhere, is thinking of me brings me great pleasure.

For the nine months since I left Fairmount, I have been working as a traveling salesman with the Kansas City Scraper Company. It is difficult but rewarding. My years in the fields and sales have prepared me well for this work, blending my knowledge of farming and business.

These metal earth-moving implements are used in road grading, railroad construction, and farming. When I arrived in Kansas City, one of the company stockholders explained that salesmen are paid on commission. I have the opportunity to increase my piggy bank far more than I ever could as a clerk in a country grocery store. Within a fortnight, I was trained as a scraper salesman. The company taught me the benefits of a single-horse-drawn steel scraper, emphasizing its cost savings, for it is ten times more efficient than a wooden plow pulled by two horses. I learned how to properly hitch the implement, adjust it, and maintain it.

I didn't expect how bone weary one could be after traveling or sleeping at boarding houses or inns every night. While I am based out of Kansas City, I travel often and have few acquaintances. I must admit, I am homesick for Fairmount.

Please give the family all my love.

Sincerely,
R. H. Wilcox

P.S. I have decided to go by my given first name, Robert. Too many people questioned my name, it being uncommon. To all my new acquaintances, I am now Robert. But for my Fairmount family, I am forever your Hillaire.

Letter from Mrs. Thixton
September 30, 1881
Fairmount, Kentucky

My Dear Hillaire,

I wish this letter contained happy tidings, yet I am afraid I have sad news to share. William Welsh passed away in August and was buried in Pennsylvania Run Cemetery. He was kin to the Welshes, whom your grandparents and mother were close to, and being one of the oldest Methodists in the area, he often joined us at our house on the Sabbath.

As you know, our brave Will now lives on Preston Street in Louisville. You should hear the stories he tells about being a patrolman for the city. He was injured in February and broke his foot, but after several weeks of bed rest, he is back on the job. On August 16, he arrested Dr. Carnachan, who attempted to burn down the Louisville Medical College. I tell you, I pray more often for my son now that he is an officer of the law than I ever did when you two played your foolish games as children.

Our harvest this year will be next to nothing unless God himself performs a mighty miracle. The entire area is suffering. I pray Mr. Graves keeps your mother's strawberry patches alive through the summer. I have enclosed the article from *The Courier-Journal* about the drought.

Your sincere friend,
Mrs. Thixton

The Courier-Journal
Tuesday, September 6, 1881
Louisville, Kentucky

The drought has dried up things in the neighborhood of Fairmount. Cedar Creek has gone entirely dry, and Floyds Fork is lower than within the knowledge of the oldest inhabitants for twenty years. Corn is literally burnt up.

Strawberries and raspberries also show feeble prospects. The last rain was on the evening of 21st July.

Robert Hillaire Wilcox Journal
March 1, 1885
Mound City, Kansas

In the five years since I left Fairmount, I have not found a close friend. Will Thixton and I grew up together, and no words were ever needed—just a look—to convey the most amusing thoughts, which would have us both laughing until tears or a good scolding from Mrs. Thixton. I have missed the camaraderie of a good friend. But that is changing.

In May of last year, I was on the train back to Kansas City from Oswego, Kansas, when I lost the twelve-inch nickel-plated model I used to demonstrate how the scraper works. Thankfully, I was on the final leg of a trip to several cities, but my, how I panicked. As I rummaged through my bags in search of the model to no avail, I conceded defeat and rested my elbows on my knees and wrung my hands. Amid my despair, a jovial voice said, "My friend, can I buy you a drink? You look as if you need one." I raised my eyes to his, and he introduced himself. "James Wayne, from Mound City." He reached out his arm and we shook hands. I declined his offer of a drink, since the memory of my father's drunken state is seared into my memory like a brand. But when he suggested a cigar, I obliged, and we went to the smoking car.

He and I were soon acquainted with one another's work. He, too, is a scraper salesman, and our paths often crossed after that since my sales territory had changed to include Mound City. He is a good sort of man, unpretentious, and raised on a farm. I do not believe he has ever met a stranger, which is an advantage in sales. He is engaged to Miss Milton, who lives in Mound City with her grandmother.

After that train ride, as soon as I arrived in Kansas City, I sent a telegram to the *The Oswego Courant* to place an ad concerning the lost scraper model. The owner of Grant's Livery Stable held it for me until I returned, and he received a handsome reward for his kindness.

Several months after that occurrence, I left the bustling city of Kansas City, where the air smells of the stockyards, a layer of dust covers every surface in dry weather, and trains that take goods back east never stop blowing their whistles. I moved to Mound City, Kansas. Returning to the country with its rolling hills and rich farmland was a balm to my soul. Mound City is less than nine hundred souls, but compared to Fairmount's population of one hundred, it has plenty to offer a man my age, without the pandemonium of the city.

Today, James and I officially secured the general agency for Slusser-McLean Scraper Company, which is based in Sidney, Ohio. By obtaining the exclusive rights to sell Slusser scrapers in this region, I have the opportunity to build a lucrative business that will sustain me, as well as a future family.

The Evening Tribune
September 16, 1885
Lawrence, Kansas

A Young Man Implicated in the Poisoning of Dora Milton, of Mound City.

The country west of Mound City was thrown into intense excitement September 11 by the announcement of the death of Dora Milton, a young lady of good family, by strychnine, the supposition being that her death was suicidal. A coroner's jury was impaneled, and their inquiry elicited a startling state of affairs, implicating J. W. Wayne, a well and popularly known young man of the neighborhood. Excitement ran high upon the streets late last night, and threats of lynching were profusely uttered. Sheriff Chandler succeeded in arresting the young man late last night at the house of one of his friends. He is now safely lodged in jail. Lynching advocates are growing less and the law will be allowed to work final vengeance if the young man is found guilty of the crime of which he is charged.

Letter to Mrs. Thixton from Robert H. Wilcox
September 30, 1885
Mound City, Kansas

My Dear Mrs. Thixton,

This is hardly a topic one should discuss with a respectable woman like yourself, but I must share my burden with someone. As you will remember from previous letters, my business partner has become a trusted friend. Oh, how I now doubt my ability to wisely judge a man. As you will read in the enclosed clipping, which has run in every newspaper west of the Mississippi, James has been arrested for the murder of his fiancée.

Yes, I was the friend James was with when he was arrested. The town had gone mad with savage intentions, and I felt I must support him in his distress with the same kindness he once offered me. His friends, who have known him since birth, turned on him. A man would hope that his neighbors, schoolmates, and acquaintances would not rush to judgment, but it seems that is not the case.

Several days ago, I ventured to the jail to question James myself. He admitted to obtaining the strychnine for Miss Milton. Imagine my surprise at his confession! I could scarcely believe what I heard. My vision grew dim, and my knees weakened to the point that I required a seat. Once I recovered, he continued to say he had no malicious intent toward Miss Milton, nor did she intend to harm herself, as the newspapers reported. James declared that Miss Milton desired to take the strychnine to end the life of the child she was carrying. His child. I barely know what to make of his reasoning since they were to be wed in one week.

On Sunday, I wandered into the nearest church in search of clarity. One of the men in attendance, a Mr. Baldwin, was kind enough to invite me to sit with his family, despite knowing I had harbored my friend the night he was arrested. The reverend's message was on Proverbs 21:2. May the Lord Almighty alone judge the heart of James Wayne. And may he give me the ability to trust again.

Yours,
R. H. Wilcox

The Blue Mound Sun
May 6, 1886
Blue Mound, Kansas

> State of Kansas vs James William Wayne, charged with poisoning Dora Milton; found guilty of murder of the first degree; sentence, "That you be hanged by the neck until you are dead, that you be confined in the penitentiary until the governor shall execute this order."

Letter from Mrs. Thixton
September 4, 1886
Fairmount, Kentucky

> My Dear Boy,
>
> I hope you don't mind this term of endearment, Hillaire, but my mother's heart breaks for you. Your friend and business partner's death sentence is horrific, but to have witnessed his execution is beyond what a moral and just man like yourself should endure. Please do not close off your heart. I pray that you will be able to trust others and eventually open your heart to a nice girl. The good Lord knows my Will hasn't found a wife yet, nor do I wish for a young woman to be wed to an officer whose life is in daily peril.
>
> I do hope you have returned safely from your trip to Ohio. I am sorry on several accounts. First, that the actions of your business partner have required you to prove that you are capable of selling the Slusser scrapers

in a respectable manner. But also, I am mostly sorry that you were so near yet couldn't stop to visit.

What a sight you would have seen! The new Fairmount Methodist Church now stands in front of the cemetery. As tradition dictates, Tom Carrithers placed a dollar bill under the cornerstone in the hope that it would bring happiness and tranquility to the church. With the meager budget, the used pews came from Cane Run Methodist Church. The white clapboard siding shines bright as a beacon of hope on Bardstown Pike. The church bell rings thirty minutes before the Sunday service begins. Mr. Thixton placed a mounting block under the big walnut tree, which is just now raining down its sweet walnuts. How nice it is for the eighty souls in the area to have a place to worship together.

You are always welcome here. Do you have plans for Christmas? How wonderful it would be to have you back with us.

Your affectionate friends,
Mrs. Thixton (and family)

Robert Hillaire Wilcox Journal
December 26, 1886
Fairmount, Kentucky

It has been good to be in Fairmount on the Thixton farm for Christmas after seven years. Mother never particularly enjoyed the holiday, despite it being her birthday. I know the day was clouded by the past for her. But the Thixtons have always celebrated the day merrily. An inch of snow covered the land as far as I could see. While Mrs. Thixton is a fine letter writer, my trip was precipitated by circumstances about which I felt more comfortable speaking with Mr. Thixton. This morning, we walked to Fairmount Falls for some privacy. The sound of our feet crunching the crisp brown leaves and icy layer of snow chased off several crimson cardinals who were roughing out the biting wind in the treetops. Once we arrived, I sat on a fallen tree trunk and stared at the crest of the falls, where dripping water had formed elongated icicles. Mr. Thixton cleared his throat to prod me into speaking my mind.

I rubbed my gloved hands together and puffed out a breath that clouded the air, as nebulous as my thoughts. I asked him if Mrs. Thixton had relayed to him the contents of my letters. He nodded in affirmation. I explained how Mr. and Mrs. Baldwin, whom I met at church, had been so kind as to have me over for Sunday dinner every weekend after church when I am not traveling. I very much enjoy their company, and that of their three sons. Yet it is their daughter, Miss Lulu Baldwin, who makes me fumble for words and causes my palms to sweat at the mere sight of her. I sounded like a schoolboy despite my twenty-eight years. Yet, I have no experience in courting. I never had much interest until my acquaintance with Miss Baldwin.

Finally, with my face feeling flushed, not from the cold but with bashfulness, I asked, "How did you know you wanted to marry Mrs. Thixton?"

"So this is the reason for your visit?" A grin broke out on Mr. Thixton's face. "My heavens, boy, you had Mrs. Thixton worried to death." He clapped his gloved hand on my back and sat next to me on the tree trunk, regaling me with how he courted "Rebecca." Mrs. Thixton's mother was a widow and lived nearby. He and Rebecca met at the Sabbath dinners when the Methodist circuit rider came to Fairmount. Since meeting privately was prohibited, the two exchanged short notes on scraps of paper, hiding them in the hollow of the beech tree we had passed on our way to the falls.

"Choose wisely, Hillaire." His eyes pierced me with a serious expression. "Work diligently so you can support a family. And don't wait until you pluck up the courage to pursue Miss Baldwin, or some other fellow will steal her out from under your nose."

Mr. Thixton headed back to the house, but I walked across Bardstown Pike to the small family cemetery where my mother and grandparents are buried. I stood in front of Mother's headstone under a naked sugar maple tree, my thoughts running awry after Mr. Thixton's words. How I wish I could ask Mother for some wisdom. I have a good income with my sales position. I believe I have chosen my affections wisely, though my past choices in friendship still haunt me. How do I find the courage to pursue Miss Baldwin? I tremble at the thought of entrusting my heart to her.

Perhaps this is the adventure I have always envisioned. Not the excitement of freedom or travel but I am beginning to believe that the greatest pursuit in life may be a wife and children and a home we can build together with deep, established roots. Yet, I hear a voice hissing my fear: that I will abandon Miss Baldwin and act more like my father than the man I hope to become. As I ponder this, I can almost hear Mrs. Thixton encouraging me with the words of St. John: "There is no fear in love; but perfect love casteth out fear."

That is enough for now. I am sitting in the living room, surrounded by the four youngest Thixtons who are tugging at my trousers and begging me to read aloud from my latest purchase, Robert Louis Stevenson's *Treasure Island*. So I will read to the children and learn from Jim Hawkins how to be brave in the face of fear and seek out my treasure, Miss Baldwin.

Letter from R. H. Wilcox to Mr. Samuel Baldwin
September 19, 1888
Kansas City, Missouri

Dear Mr. Baldwin,

My apologies for not enjoying your family's company the past several Sundays. However, I am glad to report that this long trip through Kansas, Nebraska, and Iowa has been well worth the effort. I am now in Kansas City at the fair and will return at week's end.

I must wait no longer to ask you an important question. Do you give your consent for me to request your daughter's hand in marriage? With your permission, I promise to strive to be a worthy husband and provider for Miss Baldwin.

I will anxiously await your answer upon my return to Mound City.

Yours respectfully,
R. H. Wilcox

Mound City Republic
December 6, 1888
Mound City, Kansas

Wedded.

WILCOX-BALDWIN—Nov. 29th, at the home of the bride's parents, Mr. and Mrs. Samuel Baldwin, Miss Lulu Baldwin to R. H. Wilcox, all of Mound City township.

The contracting parties to this happy union are so well and favorably known in this vicinity that were we to attempt to describe all their good qualities, or the great esteem in which they are held, we fear we would not be able to do them justice. The bride was the only daughter of our much-esteemed citizen, Samuel Baldwin. She is kind, agreeable, and affectionate as a daughter and possesses all the graces and accomplishments that go to make up the true lady and faithful wife. We believe that Robert has made a selection that he will never have cause to regret.

The groom is a young man of sterling worth. His long acquaintance and straightforward manner of doing business have won for him a good reputation. Pleasant and obliging, he is a general favorite with all. We tender to them our hearty congratulations and our best wishes for their future success and prosperity as they travel life's uneven journey together. We understand they have bought the J. G. Cash property in the southern part of the city and will soon take possession.

Letter from Robert H. Wilcox to Lulu Wilcox
December 19, 1890
San Diego, California

Dearest Lulu,

The past four weeks have been long and lonely without you by my side. I do not envy the single man who has no one waiting to welcome him home.

Business in California has been profitable. In this city of sixteen thousand, called San Diego, ranching and farming are the backbone of the economy. The contractor of a large dam at Penasquitos purchased several scrapers as they are under pressure to complete the project. The cities of El Cajon and San Diego both agreed to make purchases in order to build their infrastructure, which is sorely needed in this area as they try to prove their worth as a port city.

I desperately miss you and cannot wait to hold you in my arms again. The expectation of our little one's arrival in several months has me considering how I can, in good conscience, continue to leave you for extended periods. I pray to be an admirable father, one worthy of the title. Even if it is to provide for you and the babe, I do not believe I can be a good father if I am absent.

We will celebrate Christmas together soon.

All my love,
Robert

Letter from Robert H. Wilcox to the Thixtons
May 10, 1891
Mound City, Kansas

My Dear Thixtons,

My lovely wife gave birth to a beautiful baby girl at the end of March. Our daughter's name is Quindaro Marie. She is named after two strong women: a Wyandot woman whose name means strength in unity, and, of course, my mother. I first learned of the woman Quindaro during my residence in Kansas City, where a nearby town bears her name and served as a refuge for fleeing slaves in the days before the war. I had the honor of meeting her during my travels south of Mound City where the tribe now resides.

What a whirlwind this past month has been. While I lack sleep, my current deprivation is not as severe as my wife's, who wakes throughout the night and barely has an opportunity to take a breath during the day.

Despite our new status as parents, I am happy to say our society has not diminished. We attended a pleasant dinner party in honor of my father-in-law. In addition, my wife's uncle, Rev. John Baldwin of Cherryvale, Kansas, has been in town these four weeks. Last week, Rev. Baldwin told me of land available in the Willamette Valley of western Oregon. As you will remember, Lulu and I wintered in that area last year and found the land fertile and the region's weather more temperate than that of Kansas. With the financial hardships this area is experiencing due to crop failure and the recent droughts, the lush valleys of Oregon are appealing.

I cannot thank you enough for sending me my collection of arrowheads as well as my Great-Grandfather Graham's madstone. How could I have left such a precious keepsake—or dare I say family heirloom—at your house all these years? The newspaper printed an article about it, which I will enclose for you. Now, a fifth generation will possess the renowned madstone.

Love from all three of your Wilcoxes,
R. H. Wilcox

Linn County Republic
April 17, 1891
Mound City, Kansas

A Madstone's History

R. H. Wilcox, of this city, showed us a madstone, which he had just received from his old home in Kentucky; he having inherited it from his mother.

In 1765, a French ship was wrecked on one of the uninhabited South Sea islands, and one of the passengers, by the name of Touzalien, was left on the island alone. In his search for food, he killed a deer, and while dressing it, discovered a soft, spongy substance in the maw. Not knowing that this soft bone had any value, he left it on the ground and, in a few days, picked it up and found that the exposure to the sun had hardened it.

Four years after the shipwreck, the castaway was taken off the island by an English vessel and landed on the eastern coast of North America. He came to a place in Pennsylvania and there stopped with R. H. Wilcox's great-grandfather, a Mr. Thomas Graham. The survivor remained with Mr. Graham, and at his death gave him the stone. In 1797, Mr. Thomas Graham emigrated to Kentucky. The stone has been handed down to successive generations. Now, it is the property of Mr. Wilcox.

Mound City Republic
October 8, 1891
Mound City, Kansas

R. H. Wilcox, Sam Baldwin, and Rev. John Baldwin left with their families for Independence, Oregon, on Monday, where they will permanently locate.

Letter from Mrs. Thixton
August 22, 1892
Fairmount, Kentucky

Dear H,

How good it was to receive your letter and learn that you have settled in Independence, Oregon. My! To have procured your own grocery store with your brother-in-law Melville. The Wilcox & Baldwin Grocery and Bakery. That has quite a nice ring to it. To know you will no longer travel as a salesman but be with your wife and children gives me great joy, but surely not as much as your dear Lulu. I can still see six-year-old you in Mr. Wigginton's general store, convincing me to purchase the newly arrived canned tomatoes and baking powder. I am confident your business will thrive.

At the end of May, Mr. Thixton helped plan the Annual Floral and Fruit Exhibition of the Fern Creek Association. The weather was not ideal due to an abundance of rain earlier in the month. We had many contestants in the strawberry exhibit. However, the cherry display was not as large as it was last year due to the chilly spring. Wagons arrived from all parts of the county, and a great deal of money was profited from the auction.

The Fairmont Methodist Church arranged to have a special celebration of the Fourth of July at the Fern Creek Fairgrounds. Music and fireworks filled the air. Folks from Louisville even made the ten-mile trek to Fern Creek for the event.

Will continues to serve as deputy sheriff and finds himself in such dreadful situations. He has been present at several executions. Recently, Will arrested and interrogated a criminal who confessed that he robbed his roommate of $140. With Will's help, the unfortunate man recovered all but a few dollars.

This month, our daughter Mattie had two friends visit, and they traveled to Mammoth Cave. The three young women took the train from Louisville to Park City, then rode the Mammoth Cave Rail for the final ten miles to the park's hotel. The girls said the caves were downright cold even during the hot and humid Kentucky summer. What wonders my children have experienced!

Finally, I will boast about my dear husband. Mr. Thixton has been appointed supervisor for the 1893 assessment of Jefferson County property. The people of Fairmount, Fern Creek, and beyond think well of him. I am truly proud to call him my husband, even after thirty-nine years of marriage.

I pray you and Mrs. Wilcox enjoy the same love and admiration for each other forty years from now.

Give my love to your dear wife and daughter,
Mrs. Thixton

Letter from Lulu Wilcox to Robert H. Wilcox
June 30, 1898
Salem, Oregon

Dearest R,

I received your letter with the news of Mrs. Thixton's passing with great sadness. Although I never had the pleasure of meeting her, I am grateful that Mrs. Thixton willingly stepped into a mother's role in your life, even though she was under no such obligation.

The visit with my brother and sister-in-law in Salem has been pleasant. Melville, though he misses running the store with you in Independence, thrives as a steamboat agent with Oregon City Transportation Company.

He enjoys managing the freight logistics and schedule of the *Pomona*. Our trip from Independence to Salem on the ship went well, and I look forward to the easy return home on the Willamette River. The day cabin was modestly decorated and quite comfortable for both me and the children.

Quindaro has had a wonderful time playing with her cousin Gaynell. The two seven-year-olds incessantly chatter and play tea as if they were young women. Quindaro reads to us each evening, a trait she has inherited from you, my love. Gaynell is taking music lessons and seems to have a real talent. Fatima, such a dear sister-in-law, lends a hand when Roland gets fussy. At six months, his first teeth are coming in, and he has been out of sorts.

I pray sales continue to flourish with the West Side Trading Company. You know the dry goods business and farm implement products better than anyone in western Oregon. Your investment partners have you to thank for a successful business.

We will arrive at the dock in Independence in one week, dear. I will be standing at the bow with the children in search of you. Look for the bright yellow smokestacks of the *Pomona*. Did you know the OCT Company has been nicknamed the Yellow Stack Line for that reason?

All my love,
Lulu

JENNY SMITH

Robert Hillaire Wilcox Journal
September 1, 1903
Pendleton, Oregon

I take to my journal this evening while the house is quiet. All three children are asleep, with our youngest, Kathryn, still sleeping in our room as she is just four months old. I am grateful she is a sound sleeper for both of our sakes.

The four years we have lived in Pendleton, Oregon, have been all that I dreamed of since I was a young man. Pendleton was a stop on the Oregon Trail, but it is infamous for its history of lawless cowboys and Chinese laborers. Both are still present today.

When I was a boy in Fairmount, my imagination ran wild when I found arrowheads down by Big Run or in the orchards. I imagined scenarios of the arrowheads whirring by, intended to shoot game or engage in battle with the white settlers. In Kansas, I heard legendary stories about the Indians and even named my daughter after a Wyandot woman. But here in Pendleton, every day I work and interact with the Umatilla, Cayuse, and Walla Walla since the reservation is just a few miles from here.

Sometimes I need to remind myself that my life is not a work of fiction. How inconceivable that I might be living my boyhood fantasies!

But that is not all. My businesses are thriving. Hawley and Wilcox, where I sell some of the best local produce in our area, is flourishing. I have invested in a farming implement business with W. P. Temple, and we plan to sell automobiles in the near future. I have reinvested that money into land to grow wheat, which is generating a good profit due to the high quality and large yields that the European market needs, due to their crop failures over the past decade.

I am thankful for the success I have experienced in Pendleton, yet the distance from my wife's family has weighed heavily on me, especially of late. The two hundred and sixty miles to the Willamette Valley are easily navigated by rail and river, but Lulu spent much of the summer in Independence with her parents. My father-in-law passed last month at the age of eighty-three, and we grieve his loss. I am grateful that I have the means for Lulu and the children to travel to Independence so she could care for her father before his death. Yet, I am so very pleased to have her and the children back home.

Sadly, I have lost still another important man. Will Thixton sent me the news that his father passed away on August 16. His death comes as no surprise since he has suffered from rheumatism of the heart for several years. Even though I have not been to Fairmount in nearly seventeen years, I will miss the man. Mr. Thixton was a father to me. Unfortunately, Will was unable to attend the funeral since he was in Florida convalescing from ill health.

Since Lulu's absence, I have pondered the importance of my wife and children. And these great men's death have me contemplating my life. While I ensure my businesses profit, will my earthly accomplishments impact anyone two or three generations from now? Both my father-in-law and Mr. Thixton amply cared for their families' needs. But the men also loved their wives and children, performed their civic duty, and were men of faith. I need to invest in my family and community with the same fervor as I manage my businesses if I hope to emulate these men's examples.

Letter from Herbert Thixton
October 10, 1905
Fairmount, Kentucky

Dear Hillaire,

I wanted to pass along our sad news that my brother Will died on October 4 from tuberculosis. He had come to Fairmount to live with me six months ago, hoping that his health would improve. Since he remained unmarried, he left his belongings to me.

My brother and two sisters came from Louisville for the funeral at Fairmont Church. Will was buried in the churchyard near our parents.

You were always a dear friend to Will and my parents, even after you left Fairmount.

Sincerely,
Herbert Thixton

Robert Hillaire Wilcox Journal
January 12, 1912
Pendleton, Oregon

My eyes are heavy with sleep, but my heart feels lighter after today's meeting to address the needs of Pendleton's sick and poor. On any given day, a person walking our city streets sees men begging for the price of a meal. Our agricultural economy is dependent on farm and ranch hands and is, therefore, seasonal, as is the railroad industry. This time of year leaves many men without jobs. The damp, cold weather has people crowding into the saloons and breathing the wood- or coal-laden air, leading to sickness. The doctors and ministers in town have reported an increase in suffering. Due to these circumstances, Judge Stephen Lowell called a meeting at the Pendleton Commercial Club. In the rather raucous gathering, some citizens argued it is the churches' responsibility to feed the poor. Others offered up the ladies' aid society as a solution. Upon reflection, I suggested that the City Relief Association, first founded in the 1890s, be revived to this end. My proposal was unanimously accepted, and I was named president. With the support of other members, both men and women, I pray we can meet the needs of the least of these in Pendleton.

Days like this allow me to reflect on where I have come from and where I am now. I started in a small community in Kentucky, where I worked as a humble grocery store clerk. Until the day I left Fairmount, some people whispered about the questionable circumstances of my birth. Here, in Pendleton, all men arrive with a clean slate and an opportunity for success. And thanks be to God, I have been blessed with a loving family, a house to call my own, and profitable businesses.

And what a family I have! Lulu devotes her time to our children and often hosts the Baptist Ladies Mission Circle at our home. Quindaro's big and bold personality shined as brightly on the high school theater stage performing in *The Geisha* as it now does in society circles. She graduated from Pendleton High School two years ago and works as a stenographer. Roland, whose friends call him Joe, is a young man of fourteen and spends every moment he can at the shop working on automobiles. He is a fine mechanic. Sweet

Kathryn is eight. She seems to be musically inclined like her cousin Gaynell.

I have boasted about my family enough for now. Before heading to bed, I will sit in my wingback chair in front of the fire and read the latest dime novel about Buffalo Bill, which I picked up at the general store today. Great literature it is not, but the stories remind me of how far I have come from that young Kentucky boy who could only dream of the life that I am now living.

Robert Hillaire Wilcox Journal
September 30, 1915
Pendleton, Oregon

I sit in my room tonight recalling my conversation with Fred Beyer, a musician and piano salesman who is staying with us for the week. My niece, Gaynell, met the Beyers in Germany while she was studying violin. When the war broke out, she helped the couple book transportation to return home to St. Louis where they own a successful music business.

Earlier this evening, I handed Fred a cup of coffee before I sat in a chair as we watched the logs burn a deep orange, warming the room from the first chill of fall. Over the past few days, my family and the Beyers had enjoyed Pendleton's fifth annual Round-Up, a rodeo with cowboys, cowgirls, and Indians. More than ten thousand tourists flocked to our town for the four-day event.

"Robert, even after nine trips to Europe, the Round-Up is one of the most fascinating things Martha and I have ever seen." Fred chuckled and took a sip of coffee.

"Pendleton isn't as sophisticated as Paris or Berlin, but I guarantee you witnessed more than St. Louis society will ever see outside of a picture book."

"You are right about that." Fred crossed his leg and sipped his drink before continuing. "Most people will think my tales of cowboys and Indians are a figment of my imagination. Especially the cowgirls who race while standing on the back of a horse and buck a bull as well as any man." He lifted his eyebrows in astonishment. "Your niece must have some of the frontier blood in her since she stayed in Europe and only recently returned from her study abroad."

"Yes, she and my eldest daughter are both strong and independent women, very much like those cowgirls—even the married ones such as Bonnie McCarroll." I shook my head, wondering what man would be brave and strong enough to marry my Quindaro.

"How that woman wasn't injured amazes me."

I nodded in agreement. The Round-Up always had a few injuries, but when Bonnie's horse tossed her, she'd flown through the air before landing hard on the ground—and walked away unscathed. McCarroll had argued that the women shouldn't be required to hobble their stirrups together, a practice the men preferred to make riding easier for the women. Bonnie argued it was a dangerous practice that could lead to unnecessary injuries. Nonetheless, the event planners enforced the rule, and the cowgirl had seemingly paid the price.

Fred and I sat in the welcome silence. The hum of conversation had been swept from the house when Lulu, Kathryn, Martha, and the Beyers' son, Theo, went to the house Quindaro rentes in town. My daughter and her cousin are hosting a party that will surely earn a mention in tomorrow's newspaper. Quindaro and Gaynell often host dinners followed by rounds of Five Hundred, the fashionable card game that all the young people are playing. These affairs last late into the night, so after finishing our coffee, Fred and I headed to our respective bedrooms.

In the quiet house, I think back over the Round-Up. Hundreds of Umatilla, Cayuse, Walla Walla, and Nez Perce Indians dressed in full ceremonial apparel participated in the event side by side with white men and women. For the past several years, I have raised cattle on my six-hundred-acre ranch east of town. Well, I lease the land through the Office of Indian Affairs on the Umatilla Reservation from the Cayuse, specifically from Alice Patawa and siblings Anthony, Agnes, and Marie Redhawk. Each of the lessors, or their parents, had been allotted land under the Dawes Act.

In my grocery store, I interact daily with the people of these tribes. The reservation is a short distance from downtown Pendleton, and many work as farmhands or at the Pendleton Woolen Mills. Few choose to farm their land and prefer to lease their allotments to men like me.

In my business interactions with the Indians, I trade goods in exchange for their handiwork and artifacts as payment when cash is not available—even for "firewater," as they call liquor. I have amassed quite a collection that includes a Walla Walla beaded chieftain war shirt; a Crow war belt; a saddle blanket with intricate designs; a Cayuse tomahawk peace pipe handed down for generations; and beaded purses and moccasins too numerous to count.

I do not yet understand the thinking of these tribes. They have their land but lease it to white men. The Indians claim that they want to keep their way of life, yet exchange pieces of their civilization for everyday goods in my store.

I have obtained a happy life with my family, a home I am proud of, and have found a sense of belonging in my community. I hope I have even garnered a legacy worth passing down to generations to come. Yet these tribes seem to be losing what I have found. Are my gains at their expense? If so, how will men a hundred years from now judge me?

Letter from Quindaro Wilcox to Robert H. Wilcox
December 31, 1917
Pendleton, Oregon

Dear Papa,

My mind is restless this evening. During the past two weeks, since the announcement of my engagement to Harry, I've barely had a moment to breathe in between all of the society gatherings and wedding preparations here in Pendleton. I know this decision has surprised you, but I believe you will love Harry as much as I do. He is smart, athletic, and runs in all the best social circles.

After our wedding trip, I plan to return to Pendleton and stay in my apartment to be close to you and Mama while Harry finishes up his army training at Camp Pike in Arkansas. After three years of leadership in the Girls National Honor Guard, I will soon have my very own soldier to care for!

If I have never said this before, Papa, thank you for raising me to be a capable and determined woman. I love my work as a stenographer and leading various clubs in town. I'm grateful for my education and the life you provided for me.

Tomorrow morning, you will walk me down the aisle to become Mrs. Harry W. Butterfield, but I will always be your little girl.

Hugs and kisses,
Your Quindaro

Robert Hillaire Wilcox Journal
August 4, 1931
Ellensburg, Washington

My eyes grow dim from what the doctor tells me is macular degeneration, and reading and writing are difficult endeavors for me these days. Aging makes me feel like an arrowhead with a dulled tip; I cannot accomplish all that I wish with the precision I had in the past. Yet I have enough companionship to keep me occupied.

Last year, Lulu and I, along with Quindaro, Harry, and my grandson and namesake, Bob, moved to Ellensburg, Washington. Shortly after her marriage, Quindaro and Harry moved to Yakima for business. We followed them shortly thereafter. I retired almost a decade ago, but Harry and Quin continue to run the B&H Chevrolet automobile dealership here in Ellensburg. We all live together, and Lulu cares for Bob, getting him ready for school and such. She even teaches him to play the piano. Quindaro has a knack as an office manager and runs the company alongside Harry. I like to believe she inherited her business acumen from me.

However, I can't help but wonder if the world is ready for a woman as tenacious and assertive as she is.

I thought "Papa" was the most fulfilling title I could hold until Bob called me Granddad. When he calls me that, my heart lights up as bright as the headlights on a new Chevy driving down a dark city street. In the evenings, while Lulu fixes dinner for the five of us, Bob reads with me. Of course, I am introducing him to the adventurous classics of my youth, though they may be a bit advanced for a boy of nine years old.

Joe married a lovely young woman named Marie. They live in Los Angeles, and he, too, sells automobiles. I guess his time at the shop in Pendleton taught him not only how to fix cars but sell them. I am unsure if they don't want children or if a child was not meant to be, but they do not have any. However, they do have a beloved bulldog named Duke that they overly indulge. We might even feed Duke a few scraps of table food when we visit. But that's our little secret.

And, finally, Kathryn. Six years ago, she married George Rissberger, who works in the motion picture industry in Yakima. Their daughter Shirley is but four years old. We see them from time to time, but not nearly as much as I would like.

As I try to focus my eyes on the blurry words and pages of my journal, I am reminded of the people and places that have made me who I am today. My mother, Mary, relinquished her reputation to raise me as her child. The Thixtons took me in when I was naught but a liability. The painful memories of my father have proven that a man is not obliged to repeat the sins of his father. And from my friend, James Wayne, I learned that an honorable name is more valuable than gold. Finally, God bless Lulu's father, who demonstrated how to be a loving husband and father.

While the community considers me a successful businessman, I have discovered the true value of a man's life lies in his family. By these standards, I am the wealthiest man in all of Washington.

In the time I have left on this earth, I hope to pass wisdom on to my family; lessons as tangible as my great-grandfather's madstone, which I keep in my heirloom collection. I want my children and grandchildren to embark on grand adventures, ones as unimaginable as I have known. On second thought, I desire more than that for them. I want my descendants to experience the love of family. Adventure lasts for a moment, yet it is fleeting. A full and abundant life—one filled with family, faith, and community—this is what I want my children to attain and cling to like a cowboy or cowgirl on a bucking bronco at the Pendleton Round-Up.

THE END

ADDITIONAL MATERIAL

Author's Note

"I found a cemetery."

This is how I have begun numerous conversations over the past several years.

At a homeowner's association meeting in the spring of 2022, I learned that a cemetery was less than five hundred feet from my condo in Southeast Jefferson County, Kentucky.

The cemetery was overgrown with dense trees and foliage, and a barbed wire fence surrounded it for good measure. I couldn't see a single headstone through the vegetation. My inner Indiana Jones was piqued. I couldn't resist a good historical mystery.

A few days later, a fellow neighbor and I went on the prowl. I had to have a partner in crime since I use a wheelchair and couldn't get through the growth or over the barbed wire fence. (Yes, I confess to trespassing, but I gained permission from the owner for future expeditions.)

My neighbor could see only one headstone, but it was in decent shape. She snapped a picture on my cellphone. Surrounded by tall, dry grass and dead leaves, the timeworn stone was damaged by the elements and was scarred with a horizontal crack. But I could read a name and date: Mary Wilcox, born December 25, 1836. (Yes, the birth year is different than the story; historical records lead me to believe her birth year was probably 1834.) With Mary's name and approximate date of birth, I began my quest for Mary Wilcox's story. My only goal was to discover enough facts to approach the HOA to help care for the cemetery. But the facts—and my imagination—had so much more in store.

Two years later, some young men cleaned a second headstone in the cemetery. That's how I met Ely (Eli) Stillwell. Through convoluted and in-depth research into the Stillwells, I discovered the Graham and Stillwell connection through marriage. I now have an extensive family tree, which includes the Wilcox, Stillwell, Graham, and Sanderson families.

The more I learned about Mary and her family, the more I felt a connection with them. As I delved deeper, I began to appreciate the history of Southeast Jefferson County and see the area in a different light. The land was living and breathing. It had a history unknown to so many. And its story needed to be told.

Through my research, I connected with Vikki Kaelin, a descendant of James Graham, Thomas's younger brother. Vikki had been searching for this cemetery for over twenty years.

As I was writing Robert Hillaire Wilcox's story, I decided to follow his descendants as far as possible. I found Robert "Bob" Butterfield's obituary; he is Harry and Quindaro Butterfield's son, Robert Hillaire Wilcox's grandson. The obituary listed the names of Bob's daughter and granddaughter. My stomach dropped in both fear and anticipation. I was writing about a man with living descendants. That knowledge weighed heavily on me; it was a responsibility I didn't want to take lightly. So I did what any person would do; I Facebook-stalked Robert Hillaire Wilcox's great-granddaughter and great-great-granddaughter. And I found them.

To my surprise, Robert's great-great-granddaughter, Carly, responded immediately, even sending me a few pictures of the artifacts Robert had collected. Her mother, Ann Bucklin, had recently started researching their family history. Robert's story in Part 3—a fictional history—sprang to life in unexpected ways.

Through communication with Ann, I received more details and invaluable photos. Interestingly, I never described Robert's appearance. And I'm grateful I didn't. Ann's family pictures are a gift. The second person to read Robert's story was his great-granddaughter, Ann.

You can find the concept of legacy in each story. This was especially significant while writing about Robert. It's not only because Robert's legacy lives on through his descendants. But my dad was diagnosed with terminal stage four cancer while I wrote Robert's story. Both the Wilcox and Smith legacies dominated my thoughts. Our lives impact generations to come. I hope I have depicted the Wilcox legacy suitably and carried on the Smith legacy of reading, learning, and storytelling.

As for that little abandoned cemetery, Jack Koppel, a local cemetery expert, along with several friends, helped to clear the overgrowth. Jack cleaned and repaired the three visible headstones. The second and third headstones belong to Ely (Eli) Stillwell and his wife—and Thomas's sister—Elizabeth (Lizzie in Part 1). Jack maintains the cemetery and plans to probe for more headstones.

Historical Notes

Historical fiction. I've learned how tricky it is to balance facts with unknowns of an historical person. Every name mentioned in this book is found in historical documents. In the editing process, I had to remind myself that I was writing historical *fiction*, not a history book. The abundant, fascinating details in the articles, land records, maps, wills, and books I consulted would overwhelm a reader. I had to brutally cut people and information to have a manageable story. But if you want to dig into those details, the resources are listed below.

The one part of the story that is historically inaccurate is Thomas Thixton's presence in Fairmount in 1864. As I followed Thomas and Rebecca's story through newspaper articles, I came across Thomas Thixton's obituary. While I found a document stating that he registered with the Union Army, according to his obituary and other military records, he actually fought with the Confederate Army. Thomas was captured in October 1862 and sent to a Union prison where he remained until the end of the war.

Who was Richard Wilcox?

This is the mystery I hope to solve one day. According to Robert Hillaire Wilcox's marriage and death certificates, his father was Richard H. ("Henry") Wilcox and his mother was Mary Rousseau/Roussen. Interestingly, the Rousseaus were a prominent Louisville family at the time. Lovell Harrison Rousseau was a general in the Union Army and a lawyer and politician. He had a sister named Mary who married a "Thickstun." In addition, the name Hillaire is found in the Rousseau line. Does a connection exist between the Rousseau, Thickstun/Thixton, and Wilcox families? If I find one, you can expect another book.

Robert Hillaire Wilcox's Artifact Collection

Robert Hillaire Wilcox did, indeed, have a large collection of Native American artifacts. His great-granddaughter, Ann Bucklin, loaned the collection to the Kittitas County Historical Museum in Ellensburg, Washington. The collection includes photographs by Lee Moorhouse, a well-known photographer on the Umatilla Reservation between 1880 and 1920. According to Ann, Moorhouse was a good friend of her great-grandfather, and, thus, the photos fell into Robert's hands. Ann sold the artifacts to private collectors in 2020 due to the excessive cost of insuring the items.

Fairmount Falls

Today, Fairmount Falls is located at 9800 Thixton Lane and is owned and operated by Louisville Parks and

Recreation. The stunning waterfall still exists, yet the park is inaccessible for wheelchair users. I had a *need* to see this land that was once owned by the Thixtons. Charlene Grant, a family friend, learned I was researching the Fairmount area, and she told me that her parents, Gerald and Gladys Weber, had owned the land on which Fairmount Falls is situated from 1964 to 2002. Charlene divulged that when she and her husband, Garnett, were dating, Garnett would run to the entrance of "The Property" and leave her messages on a large boulder at the entrance. While Thomas and Rebecca Thixton's note-sharing was fictional, it was inspired by these two lovebirds.

The Webers sold the land to the city of Louisville in 2002. In a letter to the family, Mr. Weber wrote: "…We would like to see [the property] preserved in the future for coming generations." Another family legacy survives in Fairmount.

In July 2025, Luke 5 Adventures helped me hike Fairmount Falls Park with a Joëlette chair, an adaptive device made by a French company that allows two people to guide the chair over various terrains. Read more and watch a short video about my adventure at Fairmount Falls here: https://jennysmithrollson.com/what-accessible-hiking-really-looks-like-with-luke-5-adventures/

Why a Sugar Maple?

As I read through the land records, various trees are mentioned to mark the borders of the properties. When I read "sugar tree," I had to look it up, only to realize that it refers to a sugar maple. Of all the vibrant colors of trees in the fall, the bright orange of the sugar maple tree is one of my favorites. So I chose sugar maple and oak trees near the cemetery.

But in ongoing research, I discovered a deeper history of the sugar maple in Fairmount. Prior to the Civil War, William Thixton's brother, John, owned a "sugar camp." A "sugar farmer" would collect the sap of a sugar maple in wooden troughs and boil it down to produce maple syrup. I found an article from June 19, 1969, in *The Jefferson Reporter* with an interview of Everette Badgett, an eighty-year-old grandson of the man who purchased the sugar farm from Thixton. Badgett is quoted: "I remember that old camp. Little hand-hewn wooden troughs sat under each tree and the sap dropped into it…. They kept some of the sugar syrup for their own use and sold the rest of it up at the Cyclone Store in Mt. Washington. They carried it up there in barrels. They made maple candy, too. I got sick many a time from eating it."

And so we have *In the Shade of the Sugar Maple*.

Historical Accuracy

In my quest for historical accuracy, I found some wonderful resources. I began with Ancestry.com and Family Search. I have more than fifty documents from land deeds, wills, tax records, settlement books, and court records that provided historical facts. But the tidbits of information and stories I uncovered at Newspapers.com from small town newspapers brought to life the facts and revealed personal details like the Graham family madstone.

All but one of the newspaper articles in Part 3 are factual. Robert Hillaire's advertisement from September 21, 1879, is similar to an actual ad, but I modified a few details to fit the story. Due to its length, I shortened the article about Thomas Graham's madstone from the April 17, 1891, edition of the *Linn County Republic*.

Beyond the sources listed above, I wanted relevant primary and secondary sources. Mrs. Mary Dewee's journal is a gem. The descriptions of her travel through Bedford and down the Ohio are where I learned so many details about travel down the Ohio River by flatboat.

The 1858 and 1879 maps of Jefferson County, Kentucky, brought nineteenth century Fairmount and Fern Creek to life. Seeing the Graham, Wilcox, Thixton, and other familiar names I'd read in sources on these maps brought to life a sense of a community that I couldn't have created without these visual pictures.

Sitting in the Kentucky Room at the Louisville Free Public Library, I gently flipped the crumbling pages of Raymond Wheeler's history on early Fern Creek. This typewritten manuscript, bound with only a plastic cover, doesn't go back as far in history as other sources, but reading Wheeler's stories made me wish I could sit down for a long chat with him. Since this manuscript is unpublished and was disintegrating with each turn of the page, I took pictures of the document to ensure it was saved in a digital format for future generations.

John James Audubon's description quoted in an article about the 1811-1912 earthquakes inspired the earthquake scene.

Finally, I spent hours scouring details in *Fern Creek: Lore and Legacy*. So much history. Too little time. I even purchased my own copy of this out-of-print book.

To experience the beautiful details and hair-pulling frustrations of primary sources, read Mary Wilcox's last will and testament below. As you will see, these documents could use a good copyeditor.

In the name of God Amen.

I Mary Wilcox of the county of Jefferson and state of Kentucky being of sound mind and memory and considering the uncertainty of this frail and transitory life do therefore make ordain publish and declare this to be my last will and Testament that is to say that first after all my lawful debts and my funeral Expenses are paid and discharged the residence of my Estate real and personal I give bequeath and dispose of as follows.

To my son Hillaire all my real and personal Estate and as soon after my death it is my request for the land to be sold to the highest bidder and the proceeds thereof to be put to the interest until my son Hillaire is 21 years of age and it is my request that the Executor of this will be appointed guardians of my son Hillaire and to see to his Education and that he works and tries to make a living and keep him out of bad company and I further desire if Hillaire should die before he is 21 years old whatever may be left and the one that takes care of him through his sickness and after all his funeral expenses are paid and tomb stones are placed to my and his Graves the residence of my Estate it is my wish and desire shall go to the person or the one that have charge of my son Hillaire Wilcox.

I likewise make constitute and appoint Thom H Thixton to be Executor of this my last will and testament here by revoking all former wills by me made. In — whereof I hereto subscribe my name this the 13" day of May 1873.

Mary Wilcox

Acknowledgements

Where do I begin? Writing often feels lonely, but without support, this novella wouldn't exist.

Do I thank—or blame—Karen H. Richardson for encouraging me to write fiction? Thank you for the motivation, although those first steps were so very intimidating. Without you, Karen, this novella wouldn't have been written.

Liz Curtis Higgs, your love and enthusiasm for being called to write is infectious. I want to thank you for "making me" interview Mary Wilcox in June 2024 at Called to Write. That evening, you set aside time for us to do one of those ridiculous fiction-writer activities: interview a character. Yes, I rolled my eyes. But I tried, and Mary told me she liked strawberries. (And since my characters are real people, does that mean I talk to dead people?)

I'm so grateful for Mindy, Lisa, Malachi, and Aden, who were my hands and feet in researching the cemetery. Vikki Kaelin, Lynn Losh, and Melissa McGill, your genealogy skills helped untangle the twisted roots of the Graham and Stillwell families.

Carly Bucklin, thank you for responding to a stranger's message on Facebook. Ann Bucklin, I have enjoyed getting to know you and your family. Thank you for sharing your personal memories and family photographs. Your input took Robert's story to another level. I pray your family continues to carry on its amazing legacy of previous generations.

Janyre Tromp, your developmental edits taught me how to write fiction and improved the story. Kathy Burge, this makes book number three for us! Thank you for your incredible copyediting skills and attention to detail. Jenneth Leed, it's three for us too! I'm grateful for your beautiful interior formatting.

Evelyn Labelle with Carpe Librum Book Design, I'm forever grateful for a beautiful book cover. Not only did you perfectly capture the feel of the book, but you unknowingly memorialized the morning my dad passed away.

Readers, thank you for the privilege of traveling back in time with me. I hope Thomas, Susanna, Mary, and Robert live on in your memories.

Discussion Guide

1. Legacy is a core thread, from Thomas clearing land to Robert pondering his impact. What does "passing down a legacy" mean to you, and how does the family cemetery symbolize that?

2. Faith plays a subtle but steady role—Susanna's prayers, Mary's doubts during the war, Robert's reflections. Share if faith has shaped your response to hardship.

3. The move westward—from Pennsylvania to Kentucky, then Kansas, Oregon, and Washington—feels epic. What draws these characters to new frontiers, and how does it reflect the broader American Dream? Would you uproot your life for an opportunity or adventure?

4. The novella spans real history (e.g., Whiskey Rebellion, earthquakes, Civil War, Westward Expansion). How does blending fact with fiction make the story more immersive? What historical event would you want to "visit" from the book?

5. Nature isn't just a backdrop—rivers, earthquakes, and droughts shape fates. How does the environment act as a character, and what does it teach about human control (or lack thereof)?

6. Robert's "questionable origins" carry stigma, yet he rises above it. How does the book explore identity and belonging for those who are adopted or grafted into family lines?

7. If you could time-travel to one era in the book (frontier 1790s, Civil War 1860s, or Roaring '20s Oregon), which would you choose and why? What modern convenience would you miss most?

8. Fun wrap-up: If this were a movie, who would you cast as Thomas, Susanna, Mary, and Robert? What song captures the book's spirit?

Resources

Beers, D.G. and J. Lanagan. *Atlas of Jefferson and Oldham Counties* (Beers & Lanagan, 1879), in the collections of Oldham County Historical Center, https://www.oldhamkyhistory.com/1879-atlas/.

Bergmann, G. T, and Korff Brothers. *Map of Jefferson County, Kentucky: Showing the names of property holders, division lines of farms, position of houses, churches, school-houses, roads, watercourses, distances, and the topographical features of the county: Distinctly exhibiting the country around the Falls of the Ohio, including New Albany and Jeffersonville, Indiana* (Bergmann, 1858), https://www.loc.gov/item/78694303/.

Blair, John L., ed. "Mrs. Mary Dewees's Journal from Philadelphia to Kentucky." *The Register of the Kentucky Historical Society* 63, no. 3 (1965): 195–217, http://www.jstor.org/stable/23375995.

Fern Creek Women's Club. *Fern Creek: Lore and Legacy 200 Years.* 1st ed. Vol. 1 Louisville, KY, 1976.

Viitanen, Wayne. "The Winter the Mississippi Ran Backwards: Early Kentuckians Report the New Madrid, Missouri, Earthquake of 1811–12." *The Register of the Kentucky Historical Society* 71, no. 1 (1973): 51–68, http://www.jstor.org/stable/23377345.

Wheeler, Howard Raymond. *Wheeler's Notes about Early Fern Creek, Kentucky and Surrounding Areas*, unpublished manuscript, 1976, in the Kentucky Room collections of the Louisville Free Public Library.

About the Author

After sustaining a spinal cord injury at sixteen, Jenny Smith went on to receive her master's degree in counseling psychology. She has been in international and stateside support-based ministry for over twenty years. By coming alongside people with spinal cord injuries and chronic physical conditions, Jenny supports and encourages others in their physical, emotional, and spiritual health as they adapt to life with a disability.

On her website JennySmithRollsOn.com, she provides education, practical solutions, resources, and hope so people can live full and productive lives. Jenny is the author of *Live the Impossible: How a Wheelchair Has Taken Me Places I Never Dared to Imagine* and *The Journey: Discovering Emotional and Spiritual Health after Disability*.

Jenny enjoys reading (and writing) historical fiction and rows with Louisville Adaptive Rowing.

STAY IN TOUCH!

SIGN UP FOR THE
JENNY SMITH ROLLS ON NEWSLETTER.

Find me at:
jennysmithrollson.com

YouTube: JennySmithRollsOn
Facebook: JennySmithRollsOn
Instagram: jenny.smith.rolls.on

www.ingramcontent.com/pod-product-compliance
Lightning Source LLC
LaVergne TN
LVHW041644060526
838200LV00040B/1698